TO THE DEVIL, A CRYPTID

HUNTER SHEA

SEVERED PRESS

TO THE DEVIL, A CRYPTID

Copyright © 2022 Hunter Shea

WWW.SEVEREDPRESS.COM

ISBN: 978-1-922861-01-6

CHAPTER ONE

SOMEWHERE IN TEXAS

The bleating of the terrified goat rode under the constant barrage of thunder. Lightning crackled against the starless sky, throwing up strange and twisted shadows in the woods. The first patters of rain plinked off the leaves. It sounded like a monsoon was barreling their way…fast.

"What about the fire?" one of the black-robed figures asked.

"It will burn for as long as it needs to burn," replied the nude woman covered in blood and holding a heavy, leatherbound book. Her name was Lupita Saenz and she was the leader of their cult. Lupita had used a metal file to whittle her eye teeth into fangs the night before, and with the way the wind was whipping her jet-black hair, she was a vision of absolute terror.

Perhaps not for Chuck Bugna, who had had enough of an unrelenting crush on Lupita to willfully join the group of weekend Satanists on the night of their big sacrifice. He couldn't stop staring at her crimson breasts. There had been promises of a wild bacchanal when they were done. Chuck had been in charge of procuring all of the alcohol and the suite at the Hampton Inn a few towns away. The word *orgy* had been bandied about and that was not something Chuck was going to miss, even if he had to watch a goat get its throat cut. Normally an animal lover, he clung to the memory of being chased by a goat at the petting zoo when he was eight. It had traumatized him.

Yeah, well fuck that goat. Chuck looked at the goat to his left as it strained against the rope, its eyes wide and terrified with each clap of thunder and flicker of lightning. *Sorry you gotta take the fall for it, but at least you'll be serving a higher purpose.*

That higher purpose, Chuck was sure, was not the incarnation of the devil or satisfied Goat Man or some lesser demon. It would be him getting laid. *With Lupita,* if the fantasies in his head managed to play out.

He just wanted this whole part to be over and done with. With his luck, he'd get struck by lightning. A whole year of chanting HAIL SATAN for naught.

Think positive. And stop looking at the goat.

Lupita motioned for Sandra on her right to hand her the chalice. She took a huge gulp and promptly spat the cheap wine into the large campfire it had taken Chuck and Dan the better part of an hour to build.

Chuck thought the wine would make the flames roar. Instead, the bitter liquid sizzled and was quickly evaporated.

She threw her head back and looked into the roiling sky.

"It's time!"

Dylan took the book from her, dropped to his knees and held it open so she could read from it. Chuck had wanted that job, if only to get closer to a naked Lupita. She had insisted Dylan be the book bearer. For that, Chuck hated Dylan just a little bit.

"Bow your heads and repeat after me," Lupita commanded. "Amen. Everlasting life and body the of resurrection the sins of forgiveness."

The group of six Satanists around the fire intoned as one. "Amen. Everlasting life and body the of resurrection the sins of forgiveness."

When they finished, the rain started to fall in earnest. So many jagged spires of lightning sprang to life, it turned night into day for several seconds. Chuck felt his arm hairs start to rise.

The rain washed the blood (pig's blood they got from the butcher) off of Lupita's tan, taut body. Chuck licked his lips.

She continued. "The saints of communion the Church Catholic holy the Spirit Holy the in believe I!"

They responded. "The saints of communion the Church Catholic holy the Spirit Holy the in believe I!"

Saying the Apostle's Creed backwards was no easy task. They had been rehearsing it for the better part of a month. Chuck couldn't count how many times he'd said it forward in church growing up. The priests used to stop random students in the school halls to make them say it until they knew it like the backs of their dirty hands. If they could only see Chuck now.

When they finished the Apostle's Creed, Lupita began chanting in a weird language that was so guttural, Chuck worried she might choke on her own tongue. His worry didn't prevent him from ogling her.

"Get the sacrifice!" she wailed. Chuck forced his eyes to lock on Lupita's face. Her eyes showed too much white. Crazy eyes. He quickly and happily went back to looking at her chest and below.

Rosie and Harold pulled the stake the goat was tied to out of the ground and led the skittish animal closer to the fire. Sandra passed the ceremonial dagger she had ordered from some seller on Etsy to Lupita. The fire hissed as the rain pounded down. Chuck could feel the thunder in his bones. This had better be quick.

Jason Derenzis stood before the Goat Man's Bridge and took a deep breath. His leather duster kept the wind and rain at bay, but his hair was plastered to his head. The beam from his flashlight lit up the red railing and old boards that made up the abandoned bridge. It was sturdy enough. It was also the kind of place that struck terror into the hearts of children, the superstitious and simpleminded.

He was none of those things.

What he was, was pissed off at the alarming number of cats that had met their end in the woods at the other side of the Goat Man's Bridge. It had gotten so bad, people in the neighborhood no longer allowed their cats to go outside and the pet store had stopped selling them entirely. Even the animal shelter shipped them off to a cat sanctuary fifty miles away.

When Jason had gotten word that there might be a Satanic ritual tonight, he'd packed his brass knuckles and lead filled baton and headed out to the woods.

The legend of the Goat Man was too enticing for the idiot wannabe devil worshippers to pass up. For over a century, the place had been a focal point for anyone with a satyr fetish and a raging case of *outcast-itis*. The litter of their twisted fantasies and failures was a killing ground of innocent cats.

Jason loved cats.

He had six waiting for him at home.

And he was tired of reading or seeing the news reports about sacrificed felines. It ended tonight.

His boots clomped along the old bridge. He even knocked the railing several times, calling for the Goat Man to come out and play. Maybe if there *was* a monster lurking in the woods, he could rile it up to take out the latest cult of morons.

Cracking his knuckles, he thought, "If only it were that easy."

The goat seemed to know what was about to happen. It stepped up its scrabbling attempts to break free from its bonds and disappear into the woods. Rosie and Harold struggled to keep it in place. A gust of screaming wind whipped the hoods that covered their faces, exposing them to the elements.

Lupita carried on as if the heavens weren't bursting around them.

The heavens. Chuck had to stifle a chuckle. This was all anything but heavenly, just as it wasn't all brimstone and wailing souls. Lupita was as hot as she was deluded. He'd heard rumors about her terrible childhood. If even half of it was true, he wasn't surprised she had gone down this road.

What he wanted now was to get out of the rain and ditch his rain-sodden cloak. The storm had brought with it a dip in temperature, injecting a rare mild chill on a Texas night. Chuck couldn't remember the last time he'd shivered.

Could be the anticipation of what was to come at the Hampton Inn later.

"Raise your daggers!" Lupita howled over the thunder, wind and lashing rain.

Chuck fumbled within the folds of his cloak for his small dagger. He'd found it at a yard sale of all places. Lupita had consecrated all of their sacrificial weapons the night before. No, not consecrated. She'd said she had to *desecrate* them. Whatever. It made no difference to Chuck.

The cult raised their blades high. Chuck's bladder twinged at the thought that he had just made himself a human lightning rod.

"Tonight, we bow to you, the Goat Man, to hear our plea. We bring you an offering and the powers of hell to wreak havoc and show the world that you are more than just a legend. You are our grand master's unholy seed, spilled on this barren land."

Lupita was pouring it on. She writhed as she let the tip of her dagger run across her flesh, lingering on her erect nipples, then dangerously plunging down to her crotch.

When she was done, she brought it to her lips and licked the dagger with her long tongue.

Chuck responded in kind, and was grateful it was hidden by his cloak.

"We do this for you! For the destruction of man! To spit in the face of a benevolent God! For..." Lupita paused as twin streaks of lightning, immediately followed by what sounded like a sonic boom, seared their eyeballs and made their ears ring. "For chaos!"

She turned her attention to the terrified goat. Harold and Rosie managed to get it to lie on its side. The goat tried to raise its head, but Rosie, who was as big as a pro wrestler, dropped his knee on it to keep it pinned to the ground.

Lupita fell to her knees and raised the dagger high above her head. A long string of babble issued from her lips. It sounded like no language and yet every language smooshed into one.

Chuck closed his eyes. He knew she would be livid if he refused to witness the sacrifice, but this was non-negotiable for his conscience. Besides, there was no way she could see his face anyway.

The poor goat cried out, a pitiable whine that for a moment, made Chuck forget all of the horny thoughts that had controlled his reasoning over the past year.

It'll all be over in a few seconds. It's just a goat. At least Lupita didn't insist on a human sacrifice.

When Jason Derenzis spotted the hooded figures around the fire, his anger went from simmering to a full boil. Then he saw the goat, and his rage increased. Sure, there didn't appear to be any cats in peril, but a defenseless animal was in danger. Jason had grown up around these parts and was sick of these woods being infamous for being the resting place of too many animal bones to count, all of them deposited here by human wastes of space.

There looked to be six such space wasters this time, and one of them was stark naked. He didn't linger on her body. He had a girlfriend he loved with all of his heart and soul back at home. Jason was not the kind of guy who thought a little window shopping was fine, so long as you didn't touch the merchandise. Sam was more perfect than he'd ever dreamt of having in his life or deserved.

The others in the hooded cloaks looked like dime store monks. So stupid. Probably all high school kids to boot. It shouldn't take much to spook them off. Sure, most people wouldn't dream of breaking up a band of Satanists when they were outnumbered six to one. Then again, most people weren't six foot five with two Golden Gloves championships under their belt, brass knuckles and other goodies tucked in their duster.

Jason stormed toward them, shouting, "Hey!"

They either couldn't hear him over the storm, or they were more than likely tripping on shrooms or some pills to understand that the end of the asshole party was heading their way.

"Get that bitch away from the goat!"

The bitch heard him. Her eyes flashed at him, and he saw madness in them.

Then she smiled, let out a piercing wail, and drove the dagger down into the goat's neck.

Chuck's eyes flew open against his will when he heard the goat let out a gurgling gasp.

There was something else.

A man's voice in the darkness. Someone who wasn't a part of them.

Shit. I can't get caught by the cops out here with this ridiculous yard sale knife!

He turned to find the source of the voice. A huge dude wearing a long, leather duster was stomping toward them. He didn't look like a cop. More like a charged-up boxer about to enter the ring. Jason recalled YouTube clips of a young Mike Tyson, back when his fights barely lasted a round. The man was as vicious as ten pit bulls. This dude was just like that, only bigger!

"Who the hell is that guy?" Dan said.

Chuck shrugged. His feet were ready to beat a hasty retreat into the trees. Maybe they all could still meet at the Hampton Inn. Or maybe not, thanks to Duster Tyson screwing everything up.

Lupita grabbed the goat by the hairs on the top of its head and dragged the knife across its throat. A torrent of blood jetted from the growing wound. Chuck thought he was going to be sick.

The intruder was close enough now to grab ahold of the back of Rosie's cloak.

"Are you out of your fucking minds?" the man shouted. The fire reflected in his eyes. Chuck took a few stumbling steps backward.

Lupita stared defiantly at the giant man. The dagger dripped goat blood. "How dare you interrupt us!" She rose up and pointed the dagger at the man's chest. He didn't even flinch.

"Put that down before you hurt yourself." He looked around at them. "So, who wants to go to the police willingly? If you want to go the hard way, I'm actually pretty cool with that." He made it a point to stare at Rosie when he said it, picking the physical alpha and daring him to flinch.

The goat, bleeding out rapidly, rasped. The man in the duster flicked his gaze at the dying animal.

Chuck was about to run when a metallic scent in the air assaulted his nostrils and his skin pebbled with goosebumps.

A brief flash of light lit up the man in the duster, striking him down.

The explosion of light and power was so intense, Chuck felt it from the bottom of his feet as it raced through his body and rocketed to the top of his skull. The cultists were thrown about like dice. He watched in horror as Lupita was lifted into the air, disappearing up into the trees.

Chuck landed on his side, his entire body tingling, heart skipping beats.

Just before he lost consciousness, he saw the big man draped across the dying or dead goat. Steam coiled off his duster and his head. The flesh on his face had been blackened, and all of his hair was gone. The pair were surrounded by an eerie red glow.

"What...the...fu..."

CHAPTER TWO

"Take off your shirt," Henry breathlessly asked his girlfriend.

Louise, or Lou to anyone who knew her, smiled and said, "Take off *your* shirt."

Henry almost got himself tangled in his shirt as he tried to set a world speed record for undressing. He tossed it in a corner of the room and was working on the button of his jeans when Lou put a hand on his chest and shook her head. "Slow down, baby. I want to make it last."

Lou grabbed his wrists and pulled his hands over his head. "Now, I want you to keep them right there."

By the look on his face, her request was like giving a child free reign in an ice cream shop and asking him not to so much as sample a single flavor.

Henry protested, "But…"

She put a finger against his lips. "No buts. Just do what I say."

His chest might have caved a little as he acquiesced, but the lump in his jeans was operating on another level. She knew that if she let the tiger out, so to speak, she would be ravaged and Henry would be done less than a minute later. They'd only done it five times before, but this was the one where she was going to make sure she got hers.

Slowly, she undid the buttons on her shirt, revealing her favorite black, lacy bra. Henry moaned and his eyes locked onto her chest. When she saw his hands move toward them, she slapped them away. "What did I tell you?"

"Jesus, Lou, you're so goddamn hot."

She started buttoning up the shirt. "If that's the way you're going to be."

Henry went into panic mode. "No, no, no! I'm sorry. I'll keep my hands to myself. See? From now on, I'm a statue until you tell me not to be."

Lou straddled his lap, feeling his hardness against her crotch. For such a slight guy, he was a big boy down there. Big and eager and inexperienced. Not that Lou was all that proficient when it came to sex, but at least she knew how to take a breath and find ways to extend the pleasure. If she couldn't get Henry to advance from minute man status soon, she'd have to let him go. Either that or buy a vibrator to finish what he started.

Undoing the buttons once again, she rose just a bit and leaned over him, letting the tip of his nose brush against the bulging tops of her downy breasts. He moaned deeply, making her shiver. When his tongue reached out for her flesh, she pulled away and wagged her finger. "Naughty boy."

To get him centered again, she pinched his nipples as hard as she could. His body stiffened and his face went red. "Ow! Fuck that hurt."

She gave a long, lingering kiss to each nipple. "There, is that better?"

There was that moan again. "Mmmm, yeah."

Nicki Minaj was playing in the background and Lou grinded against him to the erotic beat. This was kind of fun. Her first lap dance, and she wasn't being her usual clumsy self.

Of course, she could have just bounced up and down on him and screamed, "Yeee-haa!" and Henry would have been as happy as a politician in a bank vault.

"You like that, baby?" she asked in her most sultry voice, which sounded kind of silly to her.

"Oh, God, yes."

"You want to see my body?" Lou cupped her breasts when she asked him.

Henry's eyes had glazed over. "Please."

She reached back and undid the clasp with one hand while using her other arm to push the bra down while still concealing her nipples. The bra fell onto his lap. Henry thrust his hips upward as if he were trying to penetrate her through both of their jeans.

"You can look, but remember, you can't touch."

"Uh-hunh," he said, sounding drunk and on the verge of passing out.

Oh-so-slowly, Lou let her arm drop away, revealing her dark, hard nipples. Henry was a nipple man and had told her time and time again, she had the greatest pair of nipples he'd ever seen, which was something because she knew he watched a ton of porn. Everyone she knew watched porn every chance they got.

He was breathing heavily now. "You have to let me touch them. I want you so bad, Lou."

Before he could say another word, she pulled him into her cleavage and held his head there.

Henry let out a long, wild moan. His pelvis bumped against her in rapid succession. "Oh, God, baby! I'm cumming!"

Lou pulled her chest away, saw the contented look on his face. His eyes were at half-mast and he had his post-coitus smile. She smacked his chest. "Henry!"

"What? I couldn't help it. You're so sexy, you drove me crazy."

Crossing her arms over her bare chest, Lou rolled off him and snatched her bra.

"Hey, don't get dressed," Henry protested. "Just give me, like, ten minutes and we can try again."

"Yeah, and if I'm lucky, I might be able to get my pants off before you finish that time."

She stormed into the kitchen with her bra and shirt, shrugging them both on when she was out of his line of sight.

"Why do you have to be so hot?" he called after her.

It was a stupid compliment and she wasn't falling for it. Not this time.

Well, that experiment ended in disaster. Maybe she had herself to blame.

No. Henry needed to learn to control himself. Big dick or not, she couldn't go on being sexually frustrated while dummy got to live in the afterglow and brag to his friends.

"You want to make it up to me?" she said.

"Anything."

"Get me a bottle of vodka."

She'd find one way to tamp down the burning in every cell of her body, and make Henry pay to boot. He was too young looking to buy alcohol at even the most disreputable store. But, his father was a big time drinker and his house was full of booze. The kicker was, the old man kept track of every bottle, probably every ounce. Sending Henry over to nick a bottle was his version of being asked to walk the plank.

"Don't be mad at me, Lou. I promise, the second time I'll last a lot longer. I'll knock your socks off."

She stormed back into the living room, hands on her hips. "Vodka. Now."

He looked like he was going to cry. "But…"

"You ever want to see this again," she waved her hand over her body, "You're going to have to get me drunk. And we're going to the Goat Man's Bridge to do it."

His eyes rolled to the ceiling. "That place? Aren't we a little too old to believe in fairy tales?"

"Last time we were there, you looked pretty scared to me. Let's see if you can last longer on the bridge."

The storm had passed by the time Chuck awoke. His nerves felt like they were on fire. His skin hurt. The scent of burning hair and something else – barbecue? – was heavy in the damp air.

"What the hell just happened?"

Rolling onto his side, Chuck winced from the pain. He blinked his eyes hard several times to get his vision back. When he did, he wished he hadn't.

Lupita lay in a tangled heap. Wisps of smoke danced around her charred body. The white of her eyes, larger than hardboiled eggs, were in stark contrast to her crisped flesh. Her eyes were pointed directly at him, but he knew they no longer had the ability to see. No matter, it gave him a major case of the willies. He stood up too fast, swayed a moment, and reached out to the nearest tree trunk to keep from passing out again.

It felt as if he'd been run over by a runaway tractor trailer. Chuck made sure to keep his gaze averted from Lupita's crispy corpse. Only madness lived in that corner of the woods.

Not that there were fine sights to see anywhere else.

His fellow cultists were strewn about the clearing. The fire was nothing but fizzing embers. Robed figures lay still, their bodies twisted in disturbing ways.

"Harold? Sandra?"

He stood over what he believed to be their smoking bodies. Their cloaks were singed and their faces now looked like flaking charcoal. There was no sense checking for a pulse.

Everyone was dead. So why wasn't he all fried up like the rest of them?

Maybe because I didn't believe any of this horseshit.

The thought made his heart flutter. If not believing in the whole calling upon the Goat Man to appease the Devil had saved him, did that mean there was something to it? Did the Devil take them, or did God save Chuck?

His eyes wandered over to where the goat had been slaughtered. It was gone. So was the dude in the duster.

"Are you kidding me?"

He saw that goat die. It had lost so much blood, there was no way it could just waltz off into the woods.

And that guy? He'd taken a direct hit of lightning that was so strong, it had turned almost everyone around it to pork rinds.

Maybe the lightning was so intense, it reduced them to ash.

Even though he technically knew that most likely wasn't possible, he was standing in the middle of the impossible now.

"Jesus fucking Christ."

As soon as the words escaped his lips, he looked to the sky and sputtered, "I...I'm s-s-sorry. I didn't m-m-mean to say that. Please don't b-b-be mad at me." He couldn't stop his teeth from chattering as fear of retribution rattled him to his core.

"Chuck?"

Chuck spun around, terrified, wondering where the voice had come from.

"Help...me."

A beefy hand reached up from the folds of a robe.

"Rosie?" Chuck ran to the fallen cultist. The big man, whose real name was Armand but preferred to be called Rosie, like the old time football player Rosie Greer who was in that movie where he had two heads, one of them a white racist, struggled to get up. Chuck helped him as best he could.

"Holy shit, you're alive!"

Rosie pinched the bridge of his nose and groaned. When he turned to look at Chuck, his hood dropped away, revealing a face that was half-charred. Even half of his beard was gone.

"Did it work?" Rosie asked.

Chuck pointed at Lupita's corpse. "Um, not quite the way Lupita thought it would. Something happened. I'm just not sure what. Looks like you and I are the only ones that survived the lightning strike."

"Lightning?"

"You were right next to the guy when he was hit. You don't remember?"

Rosie shook his head. His face looked terrible. And exceedingly painful. Standing close to him, Chuck detected a faint scent of grilled hot dogs wafting from Rosie's skin. He had to choke back his gorge.

Chuck took him by his arm. "We need to get the hell out of here and get you to a hospital."

"A hospital? Why?"

"You'll see when we get to the car. You think you can walk?"

A harsh, guttural braying exploded from within the darkness. Chuck's heart stopped and the blood in his veins went to sub-zero.

"The fuck is that?" Rosie said.

Heavy footsteps stomped the moist earth. Chuck could feel them through the bottom of his feet. Whatever it was, it was huge and headed their way.

"I don't think we wanna stick around and find out. Let's go!"

Chuck tried to run, practically dragging Rosie with him. The man was like an anchor, but at least he could move some. They had to settle for a stumbling jog, but at least it was putting some distance between them and the thing in the woods.

Drops of rain dripped off the trees and the swollen, winding creek of water ran noisily beneath the Old Alton Bridge, known to all the locals as the Goat Man's Bridge. Henry had parked his car in one of the store lots before the Old Alton Bridge Trail, right beneath an overhead light that gave off a yellowish glow.

Lou took a long pull from the pilfered bottle of vodka as she stood before the bridge. She offered some to her boyfriend. He shook his head. He'd been uptight ever since he'd absconded with his father's hooch.

Serves him right, Lou thought. *Maybe he'll watch some videos to learn how to keep his excitement at bay.*

She thought maybe next time they did it, she'd have him sneak off with some booze first, so his mind would be on other things. It could work.

"What is your fascination with this place?" Henry asked as he lit up a cigarette.

"What? You don't want to meet the Goat Man?"

"How many times have you and your friends been out here? Anyone ever see anything resembling a Goat Man? It's boring. Next thing, you'll be asking to play with a Ouija board."

Lou took another drink. "Ha-ha. It isn't the Goat Man you should be afraid of. It's the real-life whack jobs that hang out on the other side. That's what makes it exciting."

Henry blew out a plume of smoke. "It's exciting to run into crazy homeless people? Or better yet, loonies who go out to worship the devil and kill cats?"

Everyone in town knew all about the Goat Man, which was a fun little legend, but they worried about the way it drew cultists, outsiders and the strange, many of them doing terrible things to cats and sometimes chickens. Lou had a tabby named Drusilla that she refused to let go outside for that very reason.

"Are you afraid?" she asked Henry.

"Shit yeah. And it's not being afraid. It's being smart."

Lou stepped onto the bridge. When she got close enough to one of the red side railings, she knocked three times. The night swallowed up the small echo.

After waiting a while, she turned to Henry. "Well, the Goat Man didn't tell us to get off the bridge. Guess we're free to cross." She got to walking, not waiting for Henry to keep up.

"Oh joy, we get to go into the soaking wet woods," Henry said, hurrying after her.

They made it to the other side in one piece, crossed Old Anton Road and entered the woods proper. The earth squelched beneath their feet. It was eerily silent, the night critters having fled the storm.

Lou was starting to feel the vodka. She took a deep breath of the rain-soaked air. "You want me to hold your hand?" She knew she was being a total bitch to Henry. Sexual frustration wasn't an excuse to be so mean.

"Give me that," he said, swiping the vodka from her hand and guzzling it. "How far are we supposed to walk in this swamp? My sneakers are definitely going to be ruined after this."

"I don't know. Let's just enjoy the night."

"I was enjoying the night, back at your house. Your parents are still probably out. We can always go back."

Lou needed to make this all up to him, while still indulging herself. She plucked the bottle from him, set it down on the ground and pulled him close. "We could always go for round two, right here."

Henry looked around. "Here? It's soaking wet."

Lou smiled devilishly. "We can do it standing up. Try something different. All we need is a tree to lean against. And there are plenty of them out here."

Excitement sparked in Henry's eyes. "Really?"

"Really. Come on, let's find a sturdy tree. We're going to need it."

She led him by the hand after he picked up the vodka, taking them deeper into the woods. Sure, she could choose any random tree, but a little suspense wouldn't kill him. In fact, it might make things better.

The ground brightened and she looked up to see the clouds dissipating, revealing a nearly full moon that had been there all along. It almost made Lou want to howl.

I must be really drunk.

Henry tried stopping her as they neared several thick-trunked trees, but she wanted to keep going. If they were going to fuck out here, she needed to find some kind of clearing so they could do it under that incredible moon. She wasn't keeping track of the direction they were headed, hoping the light of the moon would guide them back.

"This looks good, baby," Henry said.

She tugged on his arm, spotting something beyond the closely packed trees. "Almost there."

They popped out of the tree line into an oblong clearing. It smelled like smoke. There were the remains of a fire about twenty feet away. The dying logs were surrounded by strange lumps on the ground.

"I think we're intruding on someone else's party," Henry whispered nervously.

He was right, but Lou was curious. "Whoever it was, it looks like they left. Let's take a look."

"What if it's one of those Satanic groups? You really want to find a dead cat?"

"No. But what are those?" She pointed at the dark shapes.

"Who cares?" Henry tugged on her arm.

She resisted. "Nut up. I just wanna see."

All thoughts of sex had been replaced by a desire to see what was in the clearing. Lou couldn't explain it. Could have been the vodka talking. She trudged to the nearest mound, letting go of Henry's clammy hand.

The mound turned out to be a person dressed like some kind of monk. She couldn't see a face, though the crisped arm and hand clutching at the grass told her she'd seen enough. Lou gasped and backpedaled from the corpse. Henry pulled up behind her, saw the body and shouted, "Oh, shit!"

Something arose from behind one of the mounds in the short distance. It grew and grew until Lou thought her breath was going to give way forever. It stood well over six feet, with a broad, blood-soaked chest, massive, muscled arms and thighs the size of Henry's torso.

That wasn't what frightened her enough to make her lose her water.

Atop its corded neck was the head of a massive goat, twin, curling horns sprouting from the sides of its shaggy head. It locked eyes on them and actually sneered.

"The Goat Man!" Lou shrieked.

Henry pushed her behind him, keeping his hands on her back. "Go, go, go!"

The Goat Man bleated with a voice that sounded unlike any goat Lou had ever heard. It was deeper, darker and full of dangerous intent.

They ran as fast as they could. The thundering footfalls of the Goat Man were right behind them.

Lou was inches from the tree line when she heard Henry hit the ground. She whipped around and saw him reaching out for her. There were tears in his eyes. She reached out to grab his hands.

The Goat Man leaped into the air, closing the gap between them with hypersonic speed. It landed on top of Henry's back. This close, Lou saw it had gigantic hooves instead of feet. Henry's spine cracked under the weight of the Goat Man. A plume of blood and bits of teeth and other things she couldn't consider shot out of Henry's mouth, splashing her ankles.

As Lou jerked away, the Goat Man dove into the back of Henry's neck and tore away a chunk of flesh. It reared its head to swallow it whole and brayed at the moon while Henry's legs and arms twitched wildly. Blood sprayed from the wound like one of the fountains in front of the Bellagio Hotel in Vegas.

Lou didn't realize she was running until she was lost in the thick woods, weeping at the sounds of the hungry Goat Man and praying it wouldn't come for her.

CHAPTER THREE

Michael Clark switched the strap to his camera case to his other shoulder. The air still smelled like ozone and his shoes were already wet. He looked to his podcast partner, Chad, and rolled his eyes. "Maybe we should do this tomorrow night when things are dryer."

Chad trudged on. "No way. I want tonight's video edited and posted by tomorrow afternoon."

"It's going to look like shit."

They came to the infamous Goat Man's Bridge, standing before the Old Anton Bridge plaque. Chad swept his hand as if he were one of those models on *The Price is Right*. "Look at it. The rain has it all slick and shiny. You couldn't shoot it looking any better. Ever notice how in movies they water down the streets when they show car scenes? Same thing here, bro."

Michael sneezed and rubbed his nose vigorously. "Plus, I think I'm coming down with something. If I get pneumonia, I'm blaming you."

Chad gave Michael's shoulder a soft punch. "Man up. It's Texas, not Alaska. You'll be fine. Just take some Benadryl when we get back to the hotel. It'll dry everything up in your head. Until then, make magic with that camera."

Sighing loud enough to be heard in Arkansas, Michael set the camera bag on one of the wooden planks of the bridge and unzipped it. There was no arguing with Chad. And as much as he hated to admit it, his podcast partner had a point. The way the moonlight glinted off the slick steel and wooden bridge couldn't have been better. Their

Monstrous Places Podcast had been trending very nicely the past year. They were actually turning away sponsors. A small shred of integrity prevented them from accepting ads for pills that made men ejaculate more or devices that helped you empty your bowels more efficiently. The money coming in was almost enough to quit their day jobs. All this just for taking weekend jaunts to cool locations where legendary creatures were said to roam.

He loved being on the beaches of Montauk, but hated the cloying heat of the Scape Ore Swamp, home of the Lizard Man. Disliking heat and humidity in general, Texas was never going to be his jam. At least it was early spring and not hot enough to fry an egg on the red steel of the Goat Man's Bridge.

While Michael set up the camera, Chad studied his notes and clipped a small microphone to his shirt. He did most of the talking on camera, though Michael had his share of air time. It was enough to get recognized in the Piggly Wiggly by his mother's house just last week. He'd even signed some autographs for the teens that had been so excited to meet him.

"This is a cute little bridge," Chad said. "Looks like something out of a scene from a Lifetime or Hallmark movie. Kinda like *The Bridges of Goat Man County, A True Love Story*."

Smirking while he attached the camera to the tripod, Michael said, "How about, *Seven Brides for Seven Goat Men*?"

Chad laughed. "Here we are making fun of the Goat Man, but when you get right down to it, this legend is all about the devil. Got a lot of Bible thumpers down here. What better way to scare people away than by coming up with tales of a half man, half goat, all fire and brimstone evil?"

"Maybe it was the guilt from hanging that freed slave. They knew they did something wrong, and came up with Satan on Earth as evidence of their sins?"

Chad whipped a pen out of his pocket and started scribbling in his notebook. "Evidence of their sins. Mint! You're not as dumb as you look."

"Gee, thanks. This coming from a guy who smoked away half his brain cells in high school."

"There's still enough gray matter to be the brains behind this operation. You about ready to go?"

Michael checked his camera and gave a thumbs up.

Chad tucked his notebook in his back pocket, smoothed his long hair back and took a deep breath while stretching his neck from side to side until it cracked. He looked into the camera, rolled his shoulders, and was about to go into his preamble about the Goat Man's Bridge, including a brief history of how it came to be given such a strange name, when a screaming girl ran onto the bridge from the other side. Chad jumped and spun around. Michael almost knocked his camera over.

"Hey!" Chad shouted, clearly unnerved.

The girl ran headlong as if they weren't even there. She brushed past Chad, knocking him into one of the side supports.

Michael saw the terrified look in her eyes and put his hands up. "Slow down. What's wrong?"

Slipping around him, the freaked out girl shrieked, "Goat Man!" Seconds later, she was gone.

"Did you get that?" Chad asked with his hand over his heart.

"How could I not?"

"That was crazy. Did she say Goat Man?"

Michael shook his head. "Screamed it more than said it."

Catching his breath, Chad chuckled. "Looks like someone's friends played a trick on her. Bet they're out there laughing their butts off."

Michael stared into the darkness beyond the bridge. "Maybe we can catch them pulling a prank. It would be cool to show the dumb stuff people do to scare one another out here."

Chad was clearly intrigued. "How do you propose we do that?"

Picking up the tripod, Michael said, "First, let's get to the center of the bridge. Then, we'll just call on the Goat Man and see if her friends do anything."

"Sweet." They ambled further onto the bridge. As Michael adjusted the tripod, Chad said, "What if it isn't her friends?"

"Then it's just some other assholes who get their kicks out of scaring teenaged girls. We'll show them it doesn't work the same with a couple of strapping dudes."

When the shot was framed as good as Michael could get it, he joined Chad in front of the camera. "You talk a little bit about the Goat Man and I'll do the knocking."

"Got it. Are we hot?"

"Already cooking."

Chad cleared his throat. "Here we are at the notorious Goat Man's Bridge down in Texas where everything is bigger, including their cryptids. At least, that's what the inhabitants of the nearby towns will tell you. The terrifying half-man, half-goat has been seen around these parts since the eighteen-hundreds, when a freed slave was reportedly hanged by a gang of racist simpletons who wanted to teach the goat herder a little lesson in white justice. Is there proof that any of this happened? Not really. But the tales of a vengeful Goat Man live on. People still come to the now closed bridge to call upon the Goat Man, waiting to either hear his gruff voice tell them to get off his bridge, or worse, show himself."

A cooling breeze whispered over the bridge.

"While Michael and I were getting ready to film, a young girl came screaming out of the nearby woods, terrified that the Goat Man was after her." Chad winked into the camera. "We're about to find out if the legendary Goat Man is near."

Michael took his cue and turned to the camera. "It's said that you call upon the Goat Man by knocking three times on the bridge. Well, if he's near, I'm pretty sure he'll hear this." He rapped three times on the steel as hard as he could. His knuckles hurt like hell, but the echo was worth it.

Michael and Chad waited a moment in complete silence, aside from the rushing water beneath them.

"I guess the Goat Man only preys on girls," Michael joked.

Chad watched in stunned silence as an enormous shadow crawled up from under the bridge, seemed to take flight for a brief moment, and came crashing down on Michael. The light from his camera illuminated the terrifying beast that pinned Michael down and proceeded to clomp his head to pudding with his black hooves.

Now Chad knew why that girl was running from the woods.

The monster stomping the life out of his friend had the lower, fur-covered half of a goat, albeit one with a gym rat's bulking legs, and the top half and arms of a body builder. What was most disturbing was the goat's head, its beard stained crimson, with curling horns big enough to smash through a car.

The Goat Man, because that's the only thing it could be, huffed human/animal sounding grunts as it smashed through Michael's rib cage with a crack that echoed into the night. It turned to Chad with eyes the color of freshly drawn blood.

Chad looked down at his decimated friend, then back at the snarling beast.

He'd always dreamed he'd be the hero should a dangerous situation arise.

Instead, he ran in the same direction as the girl had. Halfway down the trail, he realized the keys to the car were in Michael's pocket.

CHAPTER FOUR

"Please, please, please, come with me."

Tina Edwards pleaded with her best friend, Samantha Nichols, as they stood outside Samantha's apartment door.

"I don't know," Samantha said. Her hair was still wet from the shower and her stomach grumbled. She hadn't eaten since breakfast and the chicken stir fry she'd made was calling to her. "I'm really kinda tired."

"I'll buy you one of those triple espresso shot coffees with all that oat milk and shit you like." Tina nervously ran her fingers through her emerald hair. It had been bright blue just the other day. Samantha kept telling her to cool it with the hair dye before she fried her head for good.

"Work was a bitch today. And I have to get up at four to get started on the wedding cake and desserts for my gig the day after tomorrow."

"I'll help you with that. Just please help me with this."

Samantha chuckled. Having Tina underfoot in the commercial kitchen space she rented for her catering business wouldn't be any help at all. Her friend would spend more time sampling than assisting.

"He's just an old man," Samantha said.

"An old priest," Tina corrected her. "You know how priests weird me out."

As part of Tina's probation, she had to do five hundred hours of community service. One of those services was bringing food to Father Farmer. The man had been old when Samantha made her First Communion twenty years ago. She remembered the looks he used to give the mothers, like they were steaming hot cross buns at a buffet.

"Fine," Samantha said with an exaggerated sigh, knowing Tina would break her down eventually. Better to give in now and get a head start on it all. "Come in and let me throw something on."

Tina clapped as she hopped into the apartment. "You're the best." Samantha walked down the hall to her bedroom. "I love you!"

"You better."

Samantha threw on an oversized sweatshirt and sweatpants, all the better to hide her figure from Father Farmer's leering eyes. Slipping into her battered red Converse she'd had since she was a teenager, she found Tina in the kitchen eating her dinner straight from the wok. "Seriously?"

"What? You're, like, the best cook in the world. How am I supposed to resist?" Her mouth was full and chewed bits of vegetables and chicken fell to the floor.

"You're an animal. At least clean up the mess."

"I'm on it." Tina scooped the food up with a paper towel, helped herself to another forkful, and knocked over the glass of wine Samantha had poured for herself before Tina rang her doorbell.

Samantha crossed her arms and shook her head as she watched the wine expand across the tiled floor. "Remind me why I ever let you into my house."

"You love me. Remember?"

"Just step away from the mess and go start your car. I'll do this before you destroy my kitchen."

Tina kissed her on the cheek. "I'm sorry. One of these days, I won't be such a train wreck."

Samantha wondered if that day would ever come. Some people, like Tina, were destined to be a destructive force of nature. It was part of her charm. Guys thought they could either fix her, or were attracted to the sense of danger that surrounded her. Samantha loved her for who she was, warts and all, since they'd been in first grade together.

But it would be nice not to have to clean everything in her wake every once in a while.

The Goat Man looked down at the pile of blood and flesh and fabric that had just a minute ago been a man. It felt good to be free. To kill.

It dropped down to all fours and lapped up the squished brains that had leaked from the man's skull. Lapping turned to sucking, and then to loud chewing. Snuffling around in the steaming remains, the Goat Man found the exploded heart, lungs and liver, crunching rib bones to dust with its massive jaws.

When it had had its fill, it looked down the path, to where the other man had run. So had the girl.

There must be others in that direction.

More to kill.

More to feed its ravenous appetite.

The Goat Man had no idea what it was, where it had come from, or why it was here, bursting with a lust to rend and rip and chew. It was a beast of pure carnal desire. Those desires commanded it to follow the fleeing man and girl.

Its hooves clopped as it sprinted on two legs, tearing up the dirt and gravel on the winding path. It opened its nostrils wide, seeking the scent of meat. It locked onto nearby prey and increased its speed.

Lupita awoke in a chamber of blistering heat, hues of red and orange burning her eyes. She writhed in exquisite agony. The ground beneath her was colder than ice, so much so that it burned as well.

Taking in her surroundings could only be done in brief glimpses before she had to slam her eyes shut. She was most certainly no longer in the woods.

Was this hell?

She listened for the screaming of souls, detecting a lone, warbling wail, only realizing moments later that the sound was coming from her.

"Master!" she cried.

As far as Lupita could tell, she was alone in this fiery place.

She had fantasized about hell all her life, a fascination that bloomed into a true passion for all things Satanic. Even as a little girl, she knew that there would never be a place in Heaven for her. Too much had been done to or around her for any kind of benevolent forgiveness. So, she turned to the Lord's enemy, the fallen one who would most certainly welcome her with open arms.

And now she was home.

The pain was both excruciating and luxuriating. It meant everything she had done had not been in vain. If this was to be her eternity, she welcomed it with open, flaming arms. At least she was wanted someplace.

Lupita let the suffering wash over and through her. She wondered if she took a deep enough breath if she would be able to expel fire like a dragon.

There was plenty of time to experiment. An infinity of exploration.

No! a deep voice rumbled.

"Master?"

Was it Satan? Or one of his minions? Her heart, if it still functioned, felt as if it swelled at the sound.

I'll show you hell.

Lupita forced her eyes open. The wall of flame around her rose higher and higher until her orbs began to melt. She wailed until her throat ripped in half and her eyeballs sizzled and popped.

Darkness came, with Lupita tumbling into a bleak expanse of nowhere and nothing.

Lou couldn't stop sobbing as she struggled to get her key in the ignition. Her heart trip-hammered so wildly, she thought she was going to pass out. And that could not be an option. Not with that creature nearby.

She almost wept with relief when the key slammed home. She gave it a hard crank and the engine sputtered to life. Her palm was soaked in sweat. Her hand slipped off the gear shift once, twice. Lou screamed and clamped down as hard as she could on the slick knob and cranked it into drive.

Flooring the gas pedal, her tires spun on the wet blacktop of the parking lot. The car fishtailed a bit, but went nowhere.

Calm...the...fuck...down! If you don't, you're going to keep doing this Scooby Doo crap where you run in place and then the Goat Man will get you for sure!

The rubber finally got traction as she eased up a bit and the car lurched forward. There was a heavy thud and Lou yelped as something rolled over her hood and into her windshield. She jerked the steering wheel hard to the right. Whatever was on the hood slipped off and out of sight.

Anxious to get the hell out of the parking lot, she made the turn to the exit.

A man popped up from seemingly out of nowhere, waving his arms to get her to stop. His petrified face was caught in the headlight's glare. One side of his face was pebbled red from major road rash. Somehow, she managed to mash the brakes in time not to hit him. Again.

He ran to her passenger door and tugged repeatedly on the handle as he slapped his palm on the window. "Let me in! Please, let me in!"

Lou looked back at where the path started, expecting to see that awful beast come bounding out of the shadows. She turned back to the frightened, injured man, fighting within herself whether to let him in or put about a thousand miles between herself and the Goat Man.

I just left Henry back there without a second thought. If I do this to another guy, my karma's gonna be super fucked.

Her finger tapped the button to unlock the door.

"Get in!"

The man piled into the car and slammed the door. Lou hit the gas and rocketed out of the parking lot.

"You're the...the girl," the man said, his teeth chattering loud enough to be heard over the whining engine.

"Huh?"

"The one who nearly knocked us over on the Goat Man's Bridge."

She had to think a moment before the image flashed in her brain. She'd been in such a blind panic, she barely remembered, and it had just happened minutes ago. Man, she was close to losing it.

"Was that really..." the man asked.

"I think it was."

Lou checked the rearview mirror and her eyes nearly fell out of their sockets.

The Goat Man was running like a bullet train from hell out of the parking lot. "Jesus Christ!"

"What? What?" The man bounced in his seat, looking all around. When he spotted the Goat Man on their tail, he screeched at a pitch that would have made Mariah Carey jealous.

"Hold on," Lou said, gripping the wheel tight. She floored the gas pedal and zipped out of the lot and into the street. The only thing that had gone her way all day was the fact it was late and the roads were mostly empty. She sped through red light after red light, expecting to be blindsided at any moment.

"I'm Chad, by the way," her passenger said through gritted teeth. He was holding onto the strap of his seat belt as if it could save him should they smash into anything at this speed. Lou actually unclipped her belt. She'd rather die in a fiery crash than at the hands of the Goat Man.

"Lou," she shot back. "Get ready for a turn."

She cut the wheel hard and for a death-defying moment, the car lifted up onto two wheels, almost tipping over as it veered onto Smithson Avenue. It righted itself by some miracle just as Chad was ending his latest high-octave wail.

Lou made a series of similar turns, trying to get off the straight and narrow, hoping beyond hope to lose the cryptid. A quick glance out the passenger side window revealed streaks of tears on Chad's face.

"Tissues are in the glove compartment," she said, her eyes flicking from the front windshield to the rearview mirror every second. So far, no Goat Man. She wanted to weep herself.

But there was no time for that. And there was no going home. All she wanted to do was drive until the Goat Man and this whole town was well behind her.

"Look what I got," Samantha said, dangling a plastic set of rosary beads in front of Tina as she drove.

"Well, aren't you Father Farmer's little angel?"

They'd delivered the food, filling his cupboards and refrigerator. Tina had also brought him two slices of pizza from Angelo's. The aging priest had asked them to sit with him while he ate. Tina looked like she'd rather eat slugs, but community hours were community hours. The priest was nothing like the way Samantha remembered him. Old age must have whittled down his libido. He just seemed happy to have them in his presence.

"Don't be jealous," Samantha said, tucking them in the pocket of her sweats. "Not everyone aspires to be the Devil's whore."

Tina's pencil-thin eyebrow arched. "Did you just call me the Devil's whore?"

"You prefer Satan's harlot?"

"Yes. I think I do."

They burst into laughter.

"I don't see why you needed me so bad. Father Farmer was nothing but sweet."

"Yeah, to you."

The streetlights reflected off the slick surface of the road. The storm had cooled things down a bit, and they rolled down their windows, happy to shut the air conditioner off.

"For someone who is soooo tough, you can be a pretty big baby."

"Wah, wah. I just don't like church stuff."

"I don't even think that qualifies as church stuff. You brought food to an old man." Samantha stuck her arm out the window, straightened her hand and let it undulate with the wind current.

Tina tapped the ashes from the end of her cigarette out her window. "You think you could do it for me from now on and give me the hours?"

They passed by a row of closed businesses. Half the streetlights were out. It was not a place Samantha would want to walk through at this time of night.

"Sure. I'll just ask your parole officer if she's cool with it."

Tina shook her head. "You're such a dyke."

"You wish. I'd be the best woman you ever had," Samantha said with a wide grin.

"I don't know about that. Remember that girl, Gina, I told you about? The one I met in juvie?"

Samantha was about to tell her she'd heard more about Gina than she'd ever cared to know when she spotted the car careening toward them. "Tina, look out!"

Tina saw it, but it was too late. Her brakes locked and her car went into a hard spin.

Next thing they heard was the crunch of metal and shattering of glass, accompanied by a feeling of being on the whip ride at the amusement park.

CHAPTER FIVE

The vehicle that contained the focus of the Goat Man's hunger for killing picked up speed and disappeared from sight. The Goat Man stopped in the middle of the street, balled its fists and bayed at the sky.

A couple out for a post-storm walk saw and heard the devilish cryptid and ran for their lives.

What to do now?

The Goat Man was in a strange place that also seemed somewhat familiar. Its skin itched with the need to take as many lives as it could. It seethed with hatred, burned with the fires from hell to wreak havoc.

The garishly lit gas station down the street caught the Goat Man's attention. A car pulled up at a pump. People walked in and out of the mini mart.

People.

Saliva dripped in thick, shining gouts from the Goat Man's maw.

Yes. People to terrify. People to destroy.

The beast crouched down to all fours and loped toward the gas station. A car coming at it from the intersection came to a screeching halt before reversing up from the way it had come.

Picking up speed, the Goat Man lowered its head and rammed into the side of the nearest car. Its owner was holding the fuel nozzle, unaware that death was fast approaching. The steel door crumpled and the car shifted, pinning the man between it and the pump. He wailed in agony as a river of blood poured forth from his wide-open mouth. The Goat Man rose to its full height, reached across the ruined automobile and pulled the man's head off his neck with one quick and brutal swipe. It tossed his head into the street, where it was promptly run over by a speeding SUV with a crack and a splat.

The wondrous sounds of humans screeching for their lives filled the Goat Man with unmitigated pleasure. Its curved cock rose from within the folds of its long fur.

The man and woman who had pulled up to the next pump screamed and tried to pull away. The Goat Man stepped in front of the car and felt the front grill crumple around its rock-hard thigh. It leaped through the windshield, peppering the horrified couple with a cascade of safety glass a moment before ripping their throats out. Geysers of blood painted the interior of the car. The Goat Man swallowed the shreds of flesh and turned its attention to the mini mart.

The people inside were pushing objects against the glass door in an attempt to keep the Goat Man out.

With a heavy snort, the beast lowered its head and steamrolled through the door and its feeble barricade. Bleating with unbridled joy, the Goat Man made quick work of the half dozen patrons inside the store, demolishing shelves and the counter as it chased them down, stomping on heads and chests, ripping off limbs and biting off the face of a caterwauling woman.

Blood ran down the aisles of the mini mart, carrying bits of hair and flesh and bone within the tide.

A car pulled into the station, saw the blood on the windows and carnage inside, and kept on going.

The creature stepped out of the mini mart, grabbed an abandoned motorcycle that had been parked by the entrance, and threw it into one of the gas pumps. The pump burst into metallic confetti. A split second later, a column of fire blasted from the ground, reaching for the heavens.

The Goat Man's chest rose and fell rapidly. This had merely been an appetizer. It needed more. It took to the streets, instinctually knowing where to find the one that had run from the woods and the one from the bridge. It had no ability to reason why this was so. Something deep within commanded it.

Lou opened her eyes and saw a world that had gone all fuzzy and sideways. Her ears rang and there was an alarming dull ache in her chest. A night breeze flitted through the car because, she realized, all of her windows were broken. As was her steering wheel. She touched her chest, wincing from the flash of instant agony, and knew if she were to take off her shirt, there would be a bruise in the shape of her steering wheel blossoming across the tops of her breasts.

"Oooh, wow, I mean, damn that hurts."

She slowly turned her head and saw Chad picking bits of glass out of his cheek. Surprisingly, there wasn't much blood.

He looked at her and said, "You okay?"

"I…I think so. Hurts to take a breath."

Chad unclipped his seat belt. "Try not to move. Something could be broken or you could have internal bleeding. Are you cold?"

Lou let her head fall back into the headrest. "It's Texas. It's never cold."

"Stay right here. I'm going to check on the other car."

Other car?

Taking a good look around, her vision starting to snap into focus, Lou saw the car she'd hit. Two women were slumped over in the front seats.

My God. I hope I didn't kill them!

Chad stuck his head inside and was talking to the driver. She lifted her head up and faced him with a look that could curdle milk. She quickly forgot about him and tended to the passenger, who was up and holding her head in her hands after a few quick shakes.

Lou was content to watch Chad try to explain things to the, happily, living women. At least until she remembered the Goat Man. The image of the horrendous beast had her trying to start her car. The engine clicked a few times, emitted a spiral of smoke from under the hood, but refused to start.

"Fuck!" she blurted, smacking the broken steering wheel with the palms of both hands.

Her outburst got the attention of the women she'd hit. Lou managed to extricate herself from her deceased car, though not without a copious helping of pain.

"I'm so sorry," she said to the clearly agitated women. "Does your car work?"

The one with the green hair pushed her door open so fast, she knocked Chad down.

"After what you did to it?" she barked. "You fucking smashed the shit out of it, you asshole."

The passenger got out and said, "Tina, just calm down."

"Calm down? This moron nearly kills us and I'm supposed to play nice with her? No way. I'm gonna kick your ass, bitch!"

Lou braced herself for impact. Her mind calculated a way to avoid getting punched by the raging passenger – Tina – and slip away in search of a fresh set of wheels to get her out of here as fast as possible. The big problem with that plan was the possibility that she may have cracked a rib or two, plus, her head was still a bit woozy.

Chad was back on his feet and managed to hold Tina back. "It was an accident."

"She was driving like a lunatic. This isn't the fucking Indianapolis Speedway."

The driver, a pretty girl with long auburn hair who didn't look like someone who would be with the punk-looking girl, stepped between Tina and Lou.

"You want to go back to jail?" she said to Tina. "Because that's exactly what will happen if you don't take it down a notch."

Some of the air deflated from Tina's anger. She shrugged Chad off of her and didn't charge at Lou.

One less thing to worry about.

"You always let your girlfriend drive like a maniac?" Tina said.

Chad shook his head. "She's not my girlfriend."

"Can we please just get the hell out of here?" Lou pleaded.

Tina took a threatening step forward. "Oh no, you're not hitting and running."

This time, Chad got in front of Tina. "You don't understand. There's a monster chasing us. It killed my friend."

"And my boyfriend. And a bunch of people who looked like they were part of a Satanic cult or something," Lou added.

The pretty, rational one said, "Look, I know you're kind of dazed. You both clearly hit your heads. I'm going to call the police so they can record the accident and make sure they bring an ambulance."

Sirens sounded off in the distance.

It wasn't far enough away to suit Lou.

She approached the girl's car, an older Hyundai that was now facing in the opposite direction with a popped trunk hood and crumpled rear quarter panel. "Can you please see if your car will start."

Tina folded her small but muscular arms across her chest. "I'm not doing shit until the cops get here." That seemed to take her aback. She looked over at her friend. "Never thought I'd say that and mean it."

"We're not crazy," Chad said, sounding crazy. "There really is a creature out there, and it's very, very fast. This isn't a safe place for any of us."

Tina clearly wasn't impressed. Her friend looked to them with pity in her eyes.

"It's...it's the Goat Man," Lou said.

Tina snorted. "The Goat Man? Yeah, right. You guys smoke a little something out by that stupid bridge?"

"I swear to you. We're telling the truth," Lou said.

"I get it. When that bad shit hits you, you can't tell your ass from an ant hill. Just chill out."

Lou's escalating fear erupted with her screaming, "We're not on drugs and we have...to...get...the...fuck...outta...here! You hear me?" She limped to the open driver's side door and attempted to get behind the wheel. Tina grabbed her by the upper arm. Her grip made Lou cry out.

"Touch my car and you die," Tina said, seething.

"Stop it!" her friend said. She pulled Tina off of Lou. "You can't go all Tina on her."

"Oh, okay Sam, so I should just let her steal my car?"

"It's not going anywhere. Look at it."

Lou used the distraction to turn the car on. It sputtered and died.

"See?" Tina's friend said.

More and more sirens were rushing somewhere. Lou thought she smelled smoke. She shot out of the car and jogged away as best she could. "Fuck this."

"Hey!" Tina called after her. "Don't make me drag your ass back here."

A warbling, alien cry echoed down the dark and deserted street. Lou stopped in her tracks.

"What the hell was that?" Tina asked.

Chad started walking toward Lou. "We told you. It's the Goat Man. If I were you, I'd start running...now!"

"Sam?" Tina said.

"I...I don't know what that was, but I know it wasn't a Goat Man."

The bone chilling ululation happened again, only this time, it sounded closer. Lou forced her legs to run and her body to block out the pain. What sounded like the heavy clopping of hooves reverberated down the dark, deserted streets.

Lou no longer cared if those two girls were going to run or not. She was in full fight or flight mode. She wondered how many other people she'd dessert before the night was through. And if she would live to see another dawn.

CHAPTER SIX

Chuck and Rosie sat opposite one another in a booth at Tito's, a small taco shop that didn't open until ten each night, catering to the crowds of young people who frequented the nearby bars. The narrow eatery was packed with drunks. After what they'd been through, both men reveled in the light and noise and company of fellow humans.

"I think I need to go to the hospital," Rosie said. He massaged the center of his chest. Before him was a spread of six skirt steak tacos, rice, beans, fried plantains and a side of chips with guacamole. He'd barely touched his first taco. That was a concern for Chuck, who was usually afraid to get his hands too close to Rosie's meal, lest he lose a digit.

"Yeah, I thought my body would be feeling better by now. It's like my skin is on fire and every nerve is screaming." Chuck bit into a chorizo taco and couldn't taste a thing. He dropped it into the red plastic basket with disgust. "My mind, I know *that's* gonna be screwed for a long time. I mean, what the hell?" He shivered just thinking about what had happened in the woods. "Lupita's dead, man."

"They're all dead." Chuck and Rosie took furtive glances to make sure no one heard them. There was no need to worry. Inebriated babble drowned out anything they said.

"Should we tell the cops?" Chuck asked.

"Hell no! What are you going to say? Oh, we were making a sacrifice to the Goat Man to appease Satan and, well, it kinda worked, but it kinda didn't because everyone else is dead."

"We could just tell most of the truth. We were all struck by lightning."

"Wearing hoods with daggers and a book of spells."

Chuck sighed. What he wanted to do was find any way to calm his singing nerves. "I guess you're right. At least we wouldn't need to explain the goat. Jesus, all I wanted to get out of this was a chance with Lupita."

"Well, you can erase that from your bucket list. Lupita won't be riding anyone in this life. My thing is, where did the goat and that dude go?"

"I think the lightning obliterated them."

"Dumb ass. Lightning doesn't work that way. You'd need to subject a body to intense heat for a prolonged amount of time to turn them to ash, much less grains so fine they can't be seen with the naked eye."

"I guess that leaves us with only one option. We called the Goat Man forth and now it's out there, pissed."

Rosie wolfed down a taco and finished with a loud belch. The two girls behind him didn't even flinch. He made a fist and pushed it into his chest. "Lupita didn't know what she was doing. She liked to claim she came from a long line of dark brujas, but she was just a bored chick who worked at Party City who thought leading a cult would rescue her from a dull life of anonymity."

"Sounds like you've put a lot of thought into it. So why were you following her around?"

Rosie winked at Chuck as he picked onions and cilantro from his beard. "Same as you. Lupita was hot."

Chuck pushed his food to the center of the table. "I'm not hungry. Let's just go to the hospital, tell them we were struck by lightning and make sure our hearts and insides aren't fried."

Eyeing the feast he'd ordered, his usual, Rosie dipped a chip in guacamole and stuffed it in his mouth. "Okay. But we tell them we were struck in your yard. I don't want them to make any connection between us and the others."

"I'm not stupid." Chuck laid a ten-dollar tip on the table.

"We're both stupid, which is why we're in the shape we're in. Let's go."

They had to squeeze through the revelers. A party bro spilled half his beer on Chuck's shirt. The cold suds felt wonderful against his hot flesh. He almost asked the guy to dump the rest on him. Chuck was afraid to see what his skin looked like underneath his t-shirt. He'd find out soon enough at the emergency room.

Rosie was filling his hand with mints at the register by the front door when they heard the screams.

A pair of bodies struck the side of the restaurant hard enough to bust them open like cheaply made pinatas.

Another body came flying out of the air and straight through a plate glass window, taking out the two couples who, a second earlier, were about to dig into their platter of flautas.

Body after body peppered Tito's Tacos. They rained down like bloody hail. One crashed through the roof and landed on a drunk girl who had been rushing to the bathroom, in obvious need to hurl. Chuck heard her spine snap from the impact.

Pandemonium took hold of the diners. Everyone pushed to get out the doors. Rosie and Chuck were at the head of that tide of crushing humanity. Unfortunately for them, the doors needed to be pulled open. The pair were smashed against the glass like bacteria specimens under a microscope. Trapped as they were, they couldn't turn away from the nightmare as it launched the limp body of a blonde-haired woman at the restaurant. She hit the doors hard enough to splinter the glass.

Chuck and Rosie fell out of the door frames in a storm of flying glass pebbles and onto their chests as if Tito's had vomited them out. The stampede of panicked diners used their backs as doormats. Chuck watched them, between wincing in exquisite agony, as they ran to the left and right of the taco shop, careful to avoid the monster.

It only took seconds for the place to clear out. Chuck reached across to Rosie. "You alive?"

Rosie grunted as he pushed himself up, his eyes locked on the Goat Man. "I guess Lupita wasn't full of shit."

The giant satyr had run out of people to throw. It seemed satisfied to stare at the wounded men. Chuck couldn't tell if its fur was red or if it was just dipped in blood. Considering what he'd just seen, he'd choose the latter.

He struggled to get to his feet, finding it almost impossible to stand straight after the pounding his back had taken.

"Holy cow. The Goat Man is real."

For some odd reason, instead of feeling as if he were about to stroke out, a sense of calm washed through Chuck. He turned to look into Tito's and eyed the splashes of blood, the broken bodies. They were responsible for all of that. Come morning, all of those families would be devastated.

They had called forth a demon, and it had all been done because he and Rosie wanted a piece of ass.

"What do we do now?" Rosie said.

They were both too battered to make a run for it. Even on a good day, Chuck was sure they couldn't outpace the Goat Man.

Chuck rolled his neck, every bone cracking. "I guess we face the music." The Goat Man cocked its horned-head, as if trying to understand their conversation.

"I don't wanna die," Rosie said.

"What we want and what we get are usually very different things." Chuck couldn't believe the beast from hell hadn't attacked them yet. Tendrils of steam came off the Goat Man's shoulders and broad chest. It remained still as stone. "Maybe it realizes we're the ones that brought it out, or gave it life, or whatever."

"So, you think it came here to say thank you?"

"I didn't say that. But maybe there was something in Lupita's spell that said it's under our command. I mean, why else hasn't it killed us yet? Who knows what Lupita was saying? I thought the language was made up, but maybe there was something to it."

Rosie breathed heavily and wetly. It sounded as if he might have a punctured lung. Fear and adrenaline must have been the only things keeping him on his feet.

Chuck, feeling emboldened by his theory, decided to test it out.

He took a faltering step toward the Goat Man.

"You know who we are. Yes, we're the ones who called on you. Well, Lupita really was the one, but you get it."

An eerie glow emanated from the Goat Man's red eyes. Chuck swallowed, his throat so dry, he felt as if he were going to choke.

"You can't hurt us, can you?"

He took another step.

"Not a good idea, Chuck," Rosie said.

Chuck waved him off with a quick flick of his hand. He addressed the beast. "I need you to let us through."

The Goat Man sniffed the air, squinting at Chuck.

To Chuck's amazement, it stepped aside with a heavy clomp of its hoof on the pavement.

"Holy shit!" Chuck turned to Rosie. "Come on."

Rosie stood his ground, shaking his head. "No way, man." One beefy hand was on his ribs and he was stooped over. When he said no way, did he mean he couldn't walk on his own, or that he wasn't about to amble past the Goat Man?

"Yes way. Look, he's letting us go. We need a hospital more than ever." Chuck held out his hand, his back to the Goat Man. "Here, let me help you."

The sudden burst of pressure on Chuck's back and chest felt as if he'd been hit with the concentrated force of a tornado. He looked down and saw a hairy arm sticking out of his chest. In the hand at the end of the arm was a red blob that pulsated.

He looked to Rosie, who was drenched in his blood, his mouth open in an O of pure terror.

"Isss tha ma heart?" Chuck sputtered.

The arm, along with his heart, retracted. Chuck's legs gave way and he hit the ground hard, though he barely felt a thing.

Lying on his side, he watched a cloven hoof step in front of his face, and then another. Rosie raised his hands in surrender, pleading for his life. The taco Rosie had eaten earlier splattered onto the ground.

Chuck's vision dimmed, but not enough to spare him from witnessing the Goat Man tear off Rosie's arms and use them to knock his head off. Rosie's head spun end over end until it hit the edge of the roof of Tito's, rebounded and plopped onto the sidewalk, rolling until it was face to face with Chuck.

Rosie without a body and Chuck without a heart stared at one another with a dying look of realization that they were the last thing either would ever see.

CHAPTER SEVEN

Samantha watched the couple run down the block and into the night. Tina shouted a litany of threats against them, their mothers and future children. Thankfully, that's all she did. She couldn't afford getting busted for physical assault. In her case, three times was not a charm.

Peeking into Lou's ruined car, Samantha pointed out something very important to her seething best friend. "She left her pocketbook!"

Tina chewed her bottom lip with such gusto, Samantha worried she'd shred it.

"At least the police will know where to look," Samantha said, rummaging through the cheap pocketbook until she found the girl's license. "Huh, she doesn't live far from me."

"I almost want to get arrested with her so I can kick her ass in jail," Tina said, pacing in a tight circle around the front of the car.

"Well, according to her license, she is seventeen, so yeah, she's probably old enough for big girl prison, just like you."

Tina gave Samantha a bit of a side-eye, and a wry smile touched her swollen lips. "Very funny."

"Now we just need the police to actually get here."

More and more sirens sounded in the distance. There must have been a huge accident or maybe, by the smell of it, a fire that required all hands on deck.

Another wild, strange and gut churning wail came from nowhere and everywhere at once. Samantha hugged herself and shivered, spinning on her heels and seeing nothing but empty buildings.

"What the hell is that?" she said.

Even Tina looked concerned. "I don't know, but it sounded closer, right?"

"Come on, cops, we're right here." Samantha stamped her feet, feeling goosebumps rise up and down her body.

Tina grabbed hold of her arm. "Does that…does that sound like a horse?"

The definitive clop-clop of hooves on pavement was out there, but where?

"Maybe someone's horse got loose?" Samantha said.

"A sick and wounded horse, by the sound of it."

"Can horses get rabies?"

Horses were big and strong and could be mean as all get out. What would a rabid horse be like? Samantha didn't want to find out.

"I guess," Tina said.

"Maybe we should wait inside the car. With the doors locked."

"Good idea."

They piled into the car and slammed the locks down, huddling into the seats to make themselves less visible. It seemed a silly thing to do if it was indeed a horse out there, but it gave them a small bit of comfort.

"I'll get out when I see a cop car," Tina said.

Samantha didn't argue. There was no doubt that Tina was the badass in what people considered their strange and impossible relationship. That being said, Tina sounded scared, and that made Samantha even more nervous.

That animal shriek erupted again. Tina leaned over Samantha's lap and popped open the glove compartment. She took out a butcher's knife.

"You have a butcher's knife in the car?"

Tina shrugged. "You never know, Sam. Though right now, I wish I had a gun."

Faint red and blue light flashed to their left.

"Oh, thank God!" Samantha put her hand to her heart and perked up in her seat. "Maybe you shouldn't greet the police with a knife in your hands."

They heard the approaching sirens. They also heard the hoofbeats. It sounded like a race to see who would get to them first.

"I'll take my chances. I know most of the cops who work the night shift. If it's one of them, they'll understand once I explain it to them."

Tina's success with the men in blue was equal to Sam's luck with winning the lottery.

They both sighed audibly when the cruiser pulled into the intersection. The police shined their spotlight directly into Tina's car, blinding them. Tina tucked the knife between the seat and center console before she raised her hand to shield her eyes.

"Just get out of the car slowly with your hands raised so they know you don't have a weapon," Tina said.

"Thanks for the advice. Especially considering we *do* have a weapon."

They opened their doors and Tina called out, "We're the ones that were hit. The girl in the other car took off running with some guy."

A pair of officers emerged from the cruiser and inspected the massive amount of damage.

"Anyone hurt?" the tall one with the mustache asked.

"They looked more hurt than we are," Tina said.

The other cop, who was older and muscular, kept looking over the cars and said, "I'm calling for an ambulance."

"We're sore, but we feel okay," Samantha said.

"I've seen people walk away from accidents that weren't half this bad and drop dead of internal injuries minutes later. Why don't you sit on the hood of the car and just stay still? Better to be safe than sorry."

The mustached cop looked past the accident, down the street. "You hear that?"

"That a horse?"

"We don't know, but it's been making some fucking weird ass noises the past few minutes," Tina said.

The police officer took a moment to study Tina's face. "Do I know you? You look very familiar."

"I'm sure our paths have crossed."

The other cop looked over Samantha's shoulder. His hand immediately went to his gun. "What the hell?"

Samantha spun around and saw a huge shadow running down the middle of the road. Streetlights exploded, showering the air with bright sparks before winking out, moments before the shadowy figure passed them. They now knew for sure where the hoofbeats were coming from.

The only problem was that this thing was running on two legs, not galloping on four.

Pop!

Another streetlight went out.

Both cops had their guns drawn. "Get behind us," the one with the mustache bellowed. Tina grabbed Samantha and they ran away from the wreck, stopping after a dozen feet to see just what was fast approaching.

"Stop right there!"

The shadow kept coming.

"We will fire if you don't stop!"

Pop!

There was just one more streetlight left before it got to the damaged cars.

The burly cop sprinted to his cruiser and spun the spotlight a second before the streetlight blew.

Samantha screamed. Tina's fingers were like cement around her arm.

The cops opened fire.

Trapped in the harsh glare of the spotlight, Samantha watched the monster flail about as the bullets hit their marks, dead center it its muscular chest. Five holes seeped a thick ichor as black as tar.

The wounds didn't slow the monster one bit. It brought its horned head down on top of one cop's skull, cracking it open like a walnut. Brain and blood flew in every direction.

Before the other cop could shoot it at point blank range, the creature batted the weapon out of his hand. It grabbed him by the back of his neck, pulled him close and ripped his throat out. His body flailed as blood sprayed all over the beast. It bleated with what could only be described as animal glee.

"Holy shit, holy shit, holy shit!" Tina dragged Samantha with her, running down the street.

Samantha had never been so scared in her life. The visage of the monster, the Goat Man in the horrid flesh, put her system into shock. She went numb, barely able to process how she was able to run, much less breathe. Her vision clouded with more and more tears every time she blinked.

Peeking behind her, she saw the Goat Man drop the cop's body in a heap and come bounding for them.

"It's coming!" she shrieked.

"Keep running!" Tina shouted, running harder.

The clopping of hooves stopped. Samantha saw a shadow pass over their heads.

The Goat Man landed in front of them. Tina stopped and Samantha crashed into her. They fell to the pavement, tumbling until they thumped against the monster's hairy legs.

Samantha opened her mouth to scream, but nothing would come out.

Tina, ever the fighter, kicked upward into the Goat Man's groin. It didn't so much as flinch.

When its gaze bore down on them, Samantha swore she saw roiling flames in its eyes.

It snorted foul breath on them, pasting their upturned faces with the stink of death and sulfur.

Tina kicked again. "Fuck you, goat boy!"

The scream finally broke free from Samantha's throat. She let loose with every ounce of her being.

The fire in the Goat Man's eyes abated just a bit. It took a step back and grumbled, "Samantha?"

CHAPTER EIGHT

Lou and Chad ran until they came to a more residential area. Chad spotted a pair of children's bikes leaning against a house. They were small but beggars couldn't be choosers. Even though the muscles in her legs felt as if they were on fire and her chest hurt, Lou pedaled hard.

I have to get home! Mom and dad will know what to do.

Another part of her thought, *fat chance! No one knows what to do with a crazed Goat Man.* In the old tales that kids told each other and were found on the Internet, the worst the Goat Man would do is warn you to get off his bridge or, in a very rare instance, chase you out of the woods. Big deal. Nowhere was it ever mentioned that the Goat Man was inclined to killing sprees.

It had to have something to do with those bodies that she and her now dead boyfriend had found. What were they doing out there? Probably devil shit. Well, if they wanted a devil, they sure got it.

She stopped her bike. Chad kept going. Looking around, she saw a street sign for Evermore Circle. Where the hell was she?

Tires screeched as Chad hit the brakes.

"Something wrong?"

"I'm just trying to figure out where we are. We can't keep running without knowing where we're going."

They must have put a mile or two between them and the Goat Man. Was that enough to take a moment to get their bearings? Was a hundred miles even enough? Maybe it had given up the chase. It was a nice thought, but Lou wasn't taking any chances. She reached for her phone in her back pocket. The map app would tell her exactly how to get home.

"Dammit."

"What?" Chad pulled up beside her. His long hair was windblown, his complexion this side of cadaverous. Was that gray streak in his hair before? Something about him seemed very familiar.

"I lost my phone."

"No worries, I have mine." He patted his pocket, then another, and then his back pockets. "Must have fallen out somewhere back there."

"Great. I need to get home, but I don't come down this part of town very often. Shit."

"Even on a good day, I'm lost without my phone. I'd say we ask someone for directions, but it doesn't look like anyone's awake. Is it true that everyone in Texas has a gun?"

"What? No. Well, a lot of people do, but not everyone."

"Normally, I'd say we knock on some doors, see if someone can help, but I don't want to get shot."

Lou rolled her eyes. "You're an idiot. Where are you from?"

"This little town in Michigan, though I've been living in New York since the podcast started making some money."

As soon as he said podcast, Lou recalled where she knew him from. "You're on that Monstrous Places podcast."

Chad nodded, nervously looking about. "Let's talk more while we're moving, yeah?"

Lou had watched Monstrous Places from time to time, whenever she was in a paranormal TV mood and tired of the same old ghost hunting crap. Chad and Michael were clearly friends, not just two actors the studio forced together. Their show was pretty good, though it sometimes took itself way too seriously. Like the time they played that sinister music all while Chad and Michael combed the beaches of Montauk, talking about the Montauk Monster while people swam and lay in the sand, soaking up the rays.

They pedaled side-by-side. Crickets chirped around them, the blaring sirens behind them growing fainter. It was hard to believe out here in the quiet night of the suburbs that the Goat Man was on the rampage.

"Your partner, his name was Mike, right?"

"He insisted everyone call him Michael. I still can't believe he's gone." Chad sniffled, turning his head away when she took a moment to face him.

"Did you film anything in the woods earlier?"

"No. We'd just set up on the bridge when everything went south."

"My boyfriend and I were in the woods, and we came upon a bunch of dead bodies. I'm thinking they were one of those Satanic groups that go out there all the time. You think it's possible they started all this?"

Chad steered around a big rock in the road. "I though the whole Goat Man thing was ridiculous, but we get paid to film in ridiculous places. After what I've seen tonight, anything's possible."

"I don't suppose in your research you came across a way to stop the Goat Man?"

"From murdering people? Ah, no. It's not really his M.O. You're a local, what do you know about it?"

"It's just a story people tell to scare kids and bring in some tourists. I've heard at least three different origin stories about the Goat Man. So, basically, it's just a lie, which is why no one can keep track of the details."

Chad looked back. "Well, it's not a lie anymore."

They kept riding the undersized bikes, but their pace slowed considerably.

"Wait." Chad stopped, planting his right foot on the ground to steady the bike. "I can't leave Michael out there."

"He's dead. I don't think he cares."

When Lou saw the pain on Chad's face, she apologized. "What I mean is, there's no reason to go back. You want to get yourself killed?"

"I've spent the last five years searching for proof of the strange and unusual, and the second I find it, I run like a child. Shit, I'm even riding on a stolen kid's bike! No, this is wrong. That Goat Man is wrong. I know the answer is back in those woods. Can you tell me how to get to the bodies you saw?"

Lou didn't want to tell him because she didn't want to be alone.

On the other hand, she'd been kind of a shit to Henry, and it had gotten him killed. She was racking up karma points – just the bad kind.

"I'll tell you, but I'm not coming with you."

"I wouldn't let you. Now, where should I go once I cross the bridge?"

She did her best to explain how to get to the clearing in the woods. Chad nodded here and there, stopping to ask for clarification, though there wasn't much to give. When she was done, he leaned awkwardly across their bikes and gave her an even more awkward hug. "Now go, get home safe. You'll know if I make it through the night. Just check out the podcast."

Chad turned the wheel and sped off, back to where the Goat Man lived. Lou shivered. She felt terrible, letting him go like that, but she was no hero. Besides, what could she do to stop that monster?

"Nothing, Lou. Nothing." She went in the other direction, wondering if there would ever be another episode of Monstrous Places.

CHAPTER NINE

When Samantha's name came out of the monster's hairy, bloody mouth, she nearly fainted.

The Goat Man took a faltering step back, its chest heaving, gore dripping off its hands, plopping onto the cement sidewalk. One second, it was about to rip Samantha and Tina into pieces. The next, it almost looked…afraid.

Tina went to kick it again, but her foot came up short.

"It knows my name," Samantha said, her voice quivering.

Tina scrabbled backward and jumped to her feet. She tugged Samantha's arms to get her up as well. "I don't give a shit if it knows your bra size, we need to run while it's frozen like that."

She was right. The terrifying beast was indeed motionless, its eyes taking in Samantha, seemingly having forgotten all about Tina and everything else around it. She felt naked under its gaze. No, not just naked. Stripped of her skin and bones until all that was left was that intangible essence that made her who she was outside of the flesh suit bestowed upon her by her parents.

"I…I…"

"Let's go!"

She ran with Tina, throwing looks back at the Goat Man every few steps, both worrying that it would pursue them and wondering just how it knew her name.

They turned a corner and pounded feet until Tina had to stop. She leaned against a car and bent over, her hands planted firmly on her thighs. "Holy crap…I'm outta...shape. Remind me to...do more cardio...if we live."

Samantha kneaded the stitch in her side. Her heart fluttered like a hummingbird's wings, and it wasn't just because she'd sprinted for seven blocks.

"Why?" Samantha said.

"Why what? Why are we running from some ugly fucking monster? Because we don't want to get killed or eaten or whatever."

Samantha had been replaying the moment when the Goat Man said her name over and over in her head. Fine tuning it as if she were putting a recording through an audio app.

Because that voice, terrifying as it had sounded coming out of a goat's head, was not new to her. She knew it better than her own voice.

Hoping to allay her fears, she grabbed her phone and called her boyfriend. The call went to voicemail. That alarmed her. Jason was always home by this time, usually watching movies on his couch with his favorite cats, Danielle and Harris, by his side. Sometimes, she wondered if he loved his cats more than her. After sending him a brief text to call her, she tucked her phone in her back pocket and sighed.

Samantha put her hands on the sides of Tina's face and felt the tears wind down her cheeks. "Why did it sound just like Jason?"

The Goat Man remained rooted to the spot long after the women had fled. Its flesh felt too hot, as if it had been dipped in molten lava.

Its blood sang with lament at having lost the wondrous chance to rend the terrified women in two. Or three. Or many, many more.

Why had it stopped?

What had it called the woman?

For the first time since the Goat Man had erupted from the woods, it felt confused, its focus lost. It wanted to kill and instill unadulterated horror in the frail humans that populated this place.

So why not this one human?

It grew angry with itself, impotent in the face of this person and this name it could no longer recall.

Lashing out in fury, it took out a chunk of the brick façade of the nearest building. Steam coiled off its fist.

A car approached the intersection, slowing down when the driver saw the three abandoned cars.

The Goat Man charged the minivan. Inside was a family of five. When they saw the Goat Man, its head lowered so it could batter the minivan, they screamed. The driver tried to speed away, but his reflexes were too slow.

Its curved horns sent the minivan rolling until it crashed against a tree. The minivan leaked fluids and smoke. Pebbles of glass had turned the pavement into a sparkling pathway to the wounded family. The Goat Man's hooves crushed the glass into powder. It ripped the sliding side door off and cast it aside as if it were the lid of a cat food can. Inside, the children were strapped to their car seats and unconscious. The parents in the front seat were out as well, their faces red with lacerations.

Braying at the moon, the Goat Man reached in and plucked out its first victim.

The wood clearing that had been silent was now filled with the snap and pop of something stirring. A crackling noise, the sound of sturdy paper being crushed into balls, came from the mound of burned flesh. The wind shifted, blowing out the last curls of smoke rising from deep within the pile of ash.

It shifted, then pulsated for a moment, gaining volume as if something were rising up from the soil beneath. The stench that emanated from it was foul and would have slayed the olfactory senses of any living creature, had they been nearby.

Luckily for the night creatures that called this place home, they were smart enough to steer clear of the field of death. Even the crickets had fled during the height of the storm, of the awful ritual that had been performed here, never to return.

A ghostly groan wafted from the ashes, increasing in pitch until it was a scream.

The ashes coalesced, taking form slowly, and by the sound of it, painfully.

An arm black as a peat bog shot out of the quivering pile. Its flesh was nothing more than barbecued flesh, riddled with a zig-zag of cracks, and within those crevices, a pale, orange glow pulsated, like lava inching below the Earth's crust.

Another arm emerged, and the screams turned to pitiable wailing.

A neck, head and legs rose out of the miasma, burning the wet grass with the heat of an industrial boiler.

When it was complete, the deformed homunculus flopped onto its back, its limbs reaching to the onyx sky, cracked lips open wide as it caterwauled, cursing its very existence.

Lupita had preferred death to this, this abomination that she had been thrust into. She beseeched the Father of Lies to take her back, to rid her of this pain. She did not want to be here. If she was to be in agony, let it be in the home where she rightfully belonged.

Her pleas were left unanswered, and the fires of hell racked her broken body.

CHAPTER TEN

On any other night, Chad would have felt like a world class ass pedaling around on a bike that was clearly made for riders under ten. Right now, he was grateful for it.

When he was a few blocks away from where Lou had crashed the car, he banked left, careful to avoid that area. If the Goat Man was even still around. It had all the subtlety of a crashing meteor, so he felt as long as he kept his eyes and ears open, he'd be able to avoid it. With any luck, it was hurtling deeper into the town. Lord knows, there were enough sirens chirping about like a swarm of agitated locusts.

The plan was to get back to the bridge, find the keys in Michael's pockets, and check out the woods, see what he could find. He'd been a huckster for so long, wishing he were doing something that really mattered. Michael was happy to find new locations and create click-worthy videos so they could rake in the ad dollars. At first, Chad had been in lockstep with him.

But, as the years went on, and he met so many fans who desperately wanted to believe the crap they were peddling, his feelings started to change. A career of perpetuating lies was not something he had aspired to.

There was no way the world wouldn't know about the truth of the Goat Man after this. It would be captured on too many cell phones, personal security cameras and the town's own CCTV cams to be discounted as a hoax or mass hallucination. Chad didn't need Monstrous Places to prove the Goat Man was real.

But maybe he could be the one to find out how the creature came to be, and hope beyond hope, how to stop it.

The Satanic cult origin made an insane kind of sense. He knew from his research that cultists from all over came to the Goat Man's Bridge and woods beyond to gain sympathy with the devil, as Mick Jagger would have put it. Sure, the vast majority of them were hacks or just young people getting their kicks.

Maybe this one knew something the others didn't.

He had to find out.

Two police cruisers sped down the parallel road with their lights on, sirens blaring. They were followed by a fire truck and three ambulances.

The Goat Man was having itself a hell of a coming out party.

Chad was so preoccupied wondering where the first responders were headed that he failed to notice the dead bodies in the middle of the road until he ran into them. The front wheel embedded itself into the crook of a severed torso, bringing the bike to a dead stop. Chad flipped over the handlebars, landing on his back on the other side of the corpses. The breath was mule-kicked from his lungs. His eyes bugged out as he struggled to breathe. His legs kicked out and his hands balled into fists.

Mercifully, his diaphragm relaxed and that first whoosh of air instantly calmed him. He took a few breaths, each one deeper than the last, until he noticed the foul odor invading his senses.

Flipping over, he got to his feet and stared down at the tangle of limbs and other body parts.

He'd read that one of the worst smells in the world was that of freshly spilled blood. Chad could confirm that right now, though the perforated guts were also adding to the heady aroma.

Backing away, he looked up and down the street, expecting the Goat Man to be lying in wait for him.

"Gotta get the fuck outta here."

The bicycle was still in working order. Chad hopped on, never looking back at the savaged remains.

Tears blurred his vision as he made his way back to the Goat Man's Bridge.

With miles to go and a monster lurking out there somewhere, Tina and Samantha found a narrow alley to collect themselves and figure out a plan to survive the night. Tina spotted an empty bottle of Boca Chica rum and smashed it against the wall, leaving the jagged neck as a weapon. She didn't think it would do much damage against the Goat Man, but she sure as shit would try her best if it came to it.

Samantha was on the verge of hyperventilating. "How in the world could that...that thing sound like Jason? How?"

Tina grabbed ahold of Samantha's arms to settle her down. "I don't know what it sounded like. I need you to calm down. Just breathe, hold it for a few seconds, and let it out. That's right."

The truth was, Tina was just as shocked by the voice that came out of the Goat Man. It did kind of sound like Samantha's boyfriend, but in another way, it didn't. Of course, how it could talk anything like a man with that goat mouth was a miracle in itself. Right now, she didn't want to indulge her friend because it was paralyzing her.

A woman screeched, her cries quickly cut off. It sounded like it was from several blocks away. Samantha pressed herself closer to Tina.

"We just need that damn thing to move on outta here," Tina whispered. "Then I can find a car with the door unlocked, hotwire the sucker and get us the hell home."

Samantha sniffled and wiped away her tears. "It can't be Jason, can it?"

"Look, I never thought he'd make the cover of GQ, but he's no goat fucking monster."

"I just don't understand."

"Then try to focus on this. We either hunker down here and wait until dawn to make our move, or we go back out there and hope some dumbass left his car door open. Okay?"

Samantha nodded. In time, she settled down and pulled away from Tina, not that there was far to go in the alley. She toed a used condom with the tip of her sneaker. "Someone likes this alley. But I don't want to stay here all night."

Tina poked her head out, saw the coast was clear, and shifted back into the shadows. "I've done it in worse places."

"You really are an animal." Samantha flashed a weak smile.

"Yeah, well, this animal is going to keep us safe tonight. You saw the way I kicked it in the balls."

"Yes, and I saw how that thing didn't even wince."

"Not the first ball-less wonder I've come across." She took a half-step out of the alley. "Come on. We'll go down that street, hope to find a ride."

They held hands as they hurried down the street, hunched over and sticking to the shadows, which the Goat Man had made easy by blowing out the streetlights. Whenever they came across a car or truck, Tina tugged on the door handle, cursing under her breath when they were locked.

Lights were on in some of the apartments that had been built over commercial storefronts. Tina saw some people peeking from between their blinds. She wondered if the news was covering the Goat Man, and people were curious, but not enough to unlock their doors. If that was the case, for once, the general populace was not dumber than a flock of turkeys.

The crunch of crashing vehicles in the distance had them pause for a moment. Tina thought she heard someone screaming, but it could have been the wind.

Yeah, the wind, my ass.

At least it sounded far away.

It took over twenty attempts before they found an unlocked car. The old Mercury Cougar had seen better days.

"Of course," Tina said. "Whoever owns this probably prays someone steals it." She opened the driver's side door and reached across the front seat to open the passenger door. "Get in."

Samantha slammed the massive door shut. Tina slipped her head and arms under the steering wheel and got to work, using her teeth to strip the wires.

"How many cars have you stolen?"

"Enough to know what I'm doing."

There were sparks, and the ancient engine sputtered to life. Tina had to use her hand to tap the gas pedal to prevent it from stalling. Once she knew it was good to go, she settled into the seat.

"And people wonder why I keep you around," Samantha said, regaining some of her normal good humor. But Tina could detect the undercurrent of anxiety and confusion.

"Time to hit the road."

The Cougar's rear wheels spun before catching enough traction to propel the hunk of steel forward.

"I'll take you to your house," Tina said. "We can crash there and wait this thing out. Maybe we'll even get a live feed of the cops taking it down."

"I keep thinking this can't be real."

"We're gonna have the bruises tomorrow and lifelong PTSD to prove it."

Tina made a sharp turn and had to jerk the wheel the other way to avoid running over a downed motorcycle. The body of the rider lay beside it, his or her head –

impossible to tell because the helmet was still on – was propped on the roof of a nearby Honda.

"Looks like our friend has been this way. Hold on."

She took the next side street. A pair of legs jutted out from beneath a sewer cap alongside a deli. Every car on this street had been smashed to pieces. The road glittered with glass like cheap diamonds.

"Nope."

Tina tried another street. This one was filled with bloody limbs and viscera. She drove around the arms and legs, her stomach revolting when the wheel made a torso that had been halved go squish.

"What the fuck is the matter with this thing? Talk about needing anger management. I thought I was bad."

Samantha had gone unusually quiet. She stared wide-eyed at the carnage all around them.

A pair of shadows darted across the street, no doubt running to escape the madness that had come to town.

No matter where Tina went, evidence of the Goat Man's passing was strewn about like confetti after a parade. Except this confetti bled.

"Look at what it's doing to everyone," Samantha said. "We should be just like that." She pointed to an unidentifiable blob of pulverized flesh and bone. "But it wouldn't kill us. Jesus, Tina, you were even able to kick it without getting your leg torn off. If someone's going to be able to stop it, wouldn't it be us?"

Tina swerved around a police cruiser. The roof had been caved in. There were no officers in sight, living or dead. "Oh sure, two girls weighing a buck thirty each should be able to kick its ass, no sweat."

Two blocks later, they seemed to drive past the carnage. The streets here were quiet and lit, which was a good thing, because they weren't far from Samantha's apartment. Tina started working on a new plan. If the Goat Man was that close, maybe they shouldn't hole up in Sam's place. Her own rat hole of an apartment was back the way they'd come, so that was out. She checked her gas gauge.

"Shit."

"What?"

"I'm almost on empty."

There was a gas station about a quarter mile away. They could probably make it without running into big and ugly. Tina had a cousin just outside Dallas. Evan wasn't a fan of surprise visits, but he'd have to suck it up on this one.

"Recalculating," Tina said, breezing through an empty intersection and ignoring the red light.

"Where are we going now?"

"Gas first, my cousin's place second."

Samantha looked out the rear window, nervously twirling her hair between her fingers. "I just keep feeling like…"

Tina hit the brakes and the Cougar nearly went into a spin. "Oh, hell no."

Three bodies exploded out of a window, hitting the street and tumbling into parked cars. More followed. People ran out of the door of a bar across the street in a wild panic.

"Not Sully's," Tina said, her knuckles white on the steering wheel.

Tina had been drinking in Sully's since she was sixteen. The owner, an old timer named Ray (there had never been a Sully), had taken a shine to her when she'd tried to order a drink with her cheap fake ID. He'd said she reminded him of his daughter, who was a bit of a lost soul herself. Ray had passed on two years ago, but Tina still went to Sully's at least three times a week. The interior of that bar was more familiar and more of a home to her than the shit piles her mother had moved them in and out of every few months, right when the back rent was due.

The Goat Man crashed through the door, its body too big for the frame. It gripped two people by their heads, dragging them along like they were teddy bears.

"That's going too far, man," Tina said, seething. "Too…fucking…far."

She revved the engine. It stuttered for a moment but kept on running.

"Tina, don't."

Tina pinned the accelerator to the floor while the Goat Man's back was to them. Samantha yelled at her, but she couldn't discern a word her friend was saying.

Sully's. Nobody destroys my home.

The Goat Man turned just in time to see the driver's side bumper ram into its hair covered leg. Tina gripped the wheel to prevent the Cougar from spinning out of control.

The impact was deafening.

The Goat Man pinwheeled into the air.

Samantha screamed.

Tina rapped her head off the steering wheel, but it wasn't hard enough to wipe the smile from her face.

CHAPTER ELEVEN

Lou wished Chad hadn't left to go back to the Goat Man's Bridge and woods beyond it. Ever since she had realized he was on a podcast she watched from time to time, it felt almost as if she knew him. She didn't want anything bad to happen to Chad because he was a part of her life, albeit a very small part. It hurt that Michael was dead, even though he didn't get as much camera time as Chad.

It also sucked that she was now lost and alone, riding this stupid kid's bike to nowhere in particular.

Worse still were the increasing sounds of bedlam getting closer all the time. The Goat Man was like a tornado of death.

It looks like the Goat Man, but that isn't the thing people have been talking about here for over a hundred years.

She wished it *was* the legendary Goat Man. That creepy monster would still be out in the woods, lurking around the bridge and scaring teens away. That was way better than ringing up a body count that would make Henry Lee Lucas blush if he wasn't lying about killing over six hundred people.

"Hey, baby."

First the voice.

Then the shadow slipping out from between a pair of parked cars.

Lou jerked the wheel and almost fell off the bike.

The shadow stepped into the oval of light coming from the streetlamp above. It was a man with face tattoos and a scraggly beard. The orange tip of a cigarette glowed as he took a puff. His shirt was about two sizes too large for his body and his jeans bunched up down by his ankles.

"You looking for some weed?"

Lou's heart pounded. She couldn't bring herself to tell him to get lost or even get to pedaling until she could calm down.

The dealer rubbed the wiry bristles on his chin as he checked her out from head to toe. "You're pretty damn fine. A little sweaty, but I'm cool with that. If you don't have money, we can work something out." He sauntered her way, staring at her as if she were an all you can eat buffet.

Was this really happening? Lou didn't have time for this asshole's nonsense.

"You can stop right there, cheap ass Post Malone," Lou said, holding out her hand with her palm facing him. "I don't want anything from you. And if you know what's good for you, you'll go back to whatever crack house you jerk off in until everything blows over."

As if to emphasize her point, a fresh round of screams was carried by the thin breeze.

"What did you call me?" he said, oblivious to the Goat Man's melody of death in the near distance.

"I don't have time for this," she said, angling the bike away from him.

As she put her foot on the pedal, he pulled a gun from his sagging jeans and pointed it at her.

"Yeah, well, maybe I *do* have time for this. All the time in the world for a sweet bitch that needs to be broken in."

Lou hit the pedals hard, weaving as much as she could as she raced away from the psycho drug dealer. She kept her head low, panting as she desperately tried to get away from him, waiting to hear that first crack of a bullet leaving the chamber while hoping she didn't feel it as it found its mark.

Tears burned her eyes and she sped down the street, afraid to look back because how awful would that be if she turned around just in time to take a bullet to her face? The way her night was going, it was entirely possible. If she was going to die, she didn't want to end up a Jane Doe with a missing face. It was vain, sure, but Lou didn't give a rat's ass what anyone would think if they could read her mind.

Why was the world out to kill her tonight?

When she was two blocks away, she let herself exhale as she slid into the darkness thanks to a busted streetlight.

A loud crack preceded sparks firing off the chain link fence to her right.

"Shit!"

She saw the Post Malone wacko running down the street.

Lou zipped away, crossing the street and jumping the curb onto the other sidewalk. Her teeth clacked together and nipped the edge of her tongue. Her mouth flooded with the taste of dirty pennies.

Another shot rang out and sounded like it hit a car. Then another that took out a window just behind her. She swerved into the street again and rode in a wild S pattern.

Shrinking herself as best she could to present a harder target, Lou found a fresh reserve of energy and hit the afterburners. She rode blindly, so wrapped in fear that she didn't realize she was heading right for the center of the latest commotion. Lou didn't even take note of the two men who almost ran into her. Both had blood on their faces and were hitting octaves no man should ever be able to achieve.

What finally snapped her out of it was the sight of some old beater ramming into the Goat Man. The wild beast flew into the air, spinning around like a football.

Lou jammed the brakes and the bike went into a long, curving skid before sliding out from beneath her. She hit the ground with her hip and rode it as if the pavement were a luge. The pain would have been excruciating if she wasn't drop dead terrified of once again coming face to face with the Goat Man.

Why the hell can't I escape this thing?

She stopped her skid and got to her feet in a rather acrobatic move that she would normally never have been able to do. She rocked on her heels, feeling the heavy thud as the monster hit the ground hard enough to make a nearby sewer cap pop up.

The Goat Man lay on the pavement, clearly dazed.

Lou didn't want to be around when it came to. She forgot about the bike and started running.

A gunshot caught her attention.

Post Malone drug dealer was still after her. What the hell was wrong with that guy?

The Goat Man rose to his full, towering height. The murderous dealer saw the beast and fired off a couple of rounds, puncturing the Goat Man's chest. Instead of blood spitting out of the wounds, a strange, crimson-tinged vapor spilled out. Lou stopped running, intrigue overriding terror.

The vapor looked like two twisting ropes. They wrapped around the dealer's neck. His eyes bulged out of their sockets, and then quickly popped like water balloons. His mouth opened to let loose with a scream of unadulterated agony, but another red vapor rope plunged into his pie hole.

Lou watched the man's neck bulge, as if it were accommodating an Amazonian anaconda as it worked its way into his bowels.

In an instant, the vapor was gone, leaving behind the bloated, twisted, eyeless body of the dealer that was still, miraculously, on his feet.

The Goat Man and the dealer slowly turned to her.

There was just no way to stop the pee as Lou wet herself.

It looked like the two beings that had tried to murder her tonight had joined forces, and that just wasn't fair.

"Hop in!" a woman's voice shouted.

Lou saw the open door to the piece of shit car. She didn't need to be told twice. She jumped into the back seat. The door was still open as the driver peeled out.

"You okay?"

The woman in the passenger seat turned around to check on Lou.

"You?" Lou said.

The driver looked in the rearview mirror and scowled. "Of all the people."

Tina and Samantha. How was that even possible?

"You're crazy," she said to Tina. "I saw you run the Goat Man over." She eyed the door handle, wondering if she would be better on her own. This girl Tina was clearly suicidal.

"Yeah, well, when I see an opportunity, I kinda have to take a chance. Too bad I didn't at least break its leg."

Samantha said, "What are you doing here?"

Lou slumped into the seat. "Running, just like I've been doing all night. Although I don't seem to be going anywhere, except closer to that thing."

The car's engine coughed as it sped up. "Uh-oh," Tina said, her eyes flicking between the road ahead of them and the rear and side view mirrors.

"Uh-oh what?" Lou said.

"They're right behind us."

Chapter Twelve

Chad didn't know this town at all, but he had no problem finding the Goat Man's Bridge. All he had to do was follow the trail of destruction and death. He found the parking lot behind the mall area with ease and the trail to the bridge and woods beyond.

Coming to a slow stop when he saw Michael's body, Chad had to take a deep breath and psych himself up into doing what had to be done next.

First things first. I have to cover his face.

The frozen look of terror on what was left of Michael's face made Chad weak in the knees. He went to Michael's camera bag and found the light blue tarpy-thing Michael carried just in case he needed to provide some cover for the camera. He looked away as he draped it over his buddy's corpse.

"I'm sorry, man."

The smell was awful. He walked away for a moment, took a deep breath, again averted his gaze, and patted Michael down until he found his jeans pocket. He reached inside, holding his breath, desperate to find the keys to the car. He thought he had it, shifted his footing and slipped in the slick of blood and gore. Chad went down, coating his clothes and bare skin with cooling stickiness.

The rocketing gorge had him stumbling away from the corpse. Chad unleashed everything he'd eaten since landing in Texas over the side of the bridge. When he felt he couldn't possibly puke anymore, he went back to looking for the keys. His index finger looped into the keyring and it only took three hard tugs to get them out.

The moonlight bathing the bridge gave him ample opportunity to see the state of himself. He looked like he'd just taken a dive into the refuse tank in an abattoir. A briny burp surfaced, but nothing else. There was a moment when he was tempted to jump into the water below, but it passed when he realized he had more to do. He settled for taking off his shirt and wiping off the worst of it. The shirt he left on the bridge.

Before going into the woods, he ran back to the car and grabbed the tire iron from the trunk. It was the best weapon available. He also found Michael's old Iron Maiden concert t-shirt crumpled in a ball in the back seat. It had a bit of funk in the fabric, but Chad didn't mind.

He'd have to cling to any remembrances of his friend and podcaster from here on in.

"Right. Let's see if I can manage not to get myself killed," he said, tapping the end of the tire iron into his palm.

Crossing the old bridge, he shivered at the memory of calling out to the Goat Man just a few hours ago. If he only knew then what he knew now.

The woods were deathly silent. Chad knew how noisy nature could be at night. He and Michael had done their fair share of traipsing in the middle of nowhere, searching for the paranormal. Sure, the passing storm was responsible for some of the unsettling quiet, but there was something more to it. If the Goat Man had come to be out here, it was no wonder the creatures great and small had scattered. The only thing dumb enough to go back here was Chad.

It was difficult, trying to follow Lou's directions, especially when a cloud would pass over the moon and rob him of the little light he had. After a few wrong turns, he found the clearing.

And the bodies.

Sure enough, they were wearing devil worshipping cloaks straight from central casting. He wondered if they'd ordered them on Amazon or had gotten them at one of those Halloween outlets last October, saving them for the big night.

"It was a hell of a big night, alright." The sound of his voice cutting through the pall of stillness gave him a measure of comfort.

There was no need to check for pulses. These people were dead, most of them resembling burnt hot dogs.

"What were you doing out here?"

There was a stake in the ground and a few feet of rope. He found daggers and a sodden book bound in leather. "Don't touch it."

Not only was this a crime scene, that book, if it was some kind of Satanic Bible, obviously had some power. The last thing he wanted to do was make contact with such a contaminated thing.

Surveying the damage, Chad couldn't shake the feeling that he was being watched. For a moment, he froze, terrified that the Goat Man was waiting for him in the shadows.

No, that wasn't how the beast operated. If the Goat Man was near, Chad would already be dead.

Something rustled behind him. Chad spun around and saw nothing but a dead body on the ground and trees filled with darkness beyond.

"Hello?"

That was a stupid thing to do. If there was a creeper about, they sure as hell weren't going to answer. Chad yelled at characters in horror movies every time they did that, yet here he was, being a dumbass.

There was a dull snap, as if a wet twig had broken in half, to his left.

He saw nothing.

Now shuffling to his right. Grip tightening on the tire iron, he steeled himself to face…nothing.

"I'm not in the fucking mood for games."

A hot, stiff breeze wafted through the clearing. It stunk of charred meat. Chad winced and went into a coughing fit. His eyes watered from the stench.

He was so busy coughing and rubbing his eyes, he didn't notice the blackened shape reach out with a gnarled hand for his ankle.

Samantha saw the Goat Man and the bloated man sprint faster than any biped should run. There was no way the Cougar could outrace them. "Hold on!"

She braced herself, grabbing hold of the seatbelt with one hand and the dash with the other. Lou managed to snap the seatbelt buckle over her lap an instant before the Goat Man leveled its horns against the trunk.

Their heads snapped back as the Cougar lurched forward, the back end swerving left and right as Tina fought for control.

"Godammit!" Tina shouted, trying to keep the old Cougar from slamming into the parked cars on either side of the road.

Samantha, who hadn't been inside a church in more than a decade, wondered if her friend should be using the Lord's name in vain. She remembered from her days in Sunday school that that was one of the big no-nos. What was right behind them was clearly something dreamed up in hell. They didn't need to piss off the other side of this equation.

The back tires popped, the percussion loud enough to make all three girls scream as if they'd been shot. Metal grinded on asphalt as Tina willed the junker to keep going.

Problem was, the Cougar had given them all it had left. The engine made a high keening sound, like Freddy Krueger scraping his claws over a metal pipe, and simply died. Lou pushed against Samantha's seat, desperate to get out.

The Goat Man drove its fists into the trunk, crumpling the metal as if it were made of aluminum foil. The car tilted backward, tossing Tina, Samantha and Lou around, before settling back down with a jaw breaking bounce.

Staying in the car was not an option. Samantha and Tina threw their doors open and scrambled out. Lou knocked into Samantha in her panic.

The Goat Man leaped onto the car, galloping over its busted hulk. The red man followed suit, though he was much less frightening to look at. In fact, he resembled a fat lobster, one that had been overcooked in the microwave and was about to pop.

Samantha knew there was no way they could get away from the two beasts while on foot.

Despite Tina and Lou yanking on her arms, she stayed her ground, bravely looking into the Goat Man's burning eyes. Its nostrils flared and smoke curled out of the twin pits. It stopped its advance, remaining on the now crumpled hood.

"Why are you doing this to us?" Samantha asked it in not her most confident tone.

"We have to run," Tina said.

"Are you out of your freaking mind?" Lou said.

Samantha remained resolute. "No. You're out of your mind if you think we can outrun them."

The Goat Man looked down at her, studying her. Samantha felt as if she were being flayed open.

And just like before, it said in its gravely voice, "S...Sambeebay?"

In that instant, she knew.

Only one person in this world called her Beebay. Just as she was the only person who lovingly referred to him as BearJay.

"Jason?"

The Goat Man rocked on its heels. After all its rampaging, it had been nearly knocked down by one word.

Which meant Samantha was right.

"No way," Tina said behind her. "That can't be. I mean, that can't be Jason."

Samantha couldn't even detect her own heart beating. She felt trapped in amber, frozen in time in the face of the impossible. "I know. But somehow...it is."

The bloated red demon took a menacing step toward them. The Goat Man stopped him by taking a swipe at his chest and knocking him off his feet.

"You know that thing?" Lou said incredulously.

Samantha's vision shimmered with tears. "He's my...my boyfriend."

There were more sirens in the distance. They appeared to be coming their way.

"There's no way you're dating that monster," Lou said.

Samantha dreamily answered her, never taking her eyes off the creature that was somehow also Jason. "He's no monster. I mean, Jason isn't a monster. He takes spiders and flies out of his apartment rather than kill them."

"It's true," Tina said. "He's kind of a big pussy."

Samantha took a daring step forward. "Jason? What happened to you? How did you end up like this?"

The Goat Man/Jason clenched and unclenched his fists, clearly at war with himself. One second, he looked like he wanted to smash her like a whack a mole, the next, she felt the confusion and recognition washing off of him in waves. It was clearly dangerous, engaging him like this. Samantha could get them all killed. Not that they weren't already in mortal danger.

Or, if she could somehow get Jason to take control, she could save not just them, but what was left of the town.

"Tell me, BearJay, how did this happen?"

His lips curled back, revealing sharp, yellow teeth.

Samantha took a stuttering breath, but remained as calm as she could. "You don't want to kill me. I know that, and you know that."

"I don't know about you and me, though," Lou said under her breath to Tina.

The red man, snarling like a hungry dog, leaped to his feet to attack Samantha. The Goat Man snatched him in mid-air by the back of his neck. The women recoiled at the snapping of his bones. He fell at her feet in a motionless heap, yet still very much alive. His lips pulled back and his tongue flicked out like a snake. Samantha shuffled back, knowing she would pass out if that nasty tongue so much as grazed her ankle.

"Jason, what can I do? Please, you have to help me so I can help you."

"S-Samantha."

She reached out to touch the Goat Man. None of this made any sense, but she knew Jason was in there and she would do anything to free him. Jason had once saved her life when she was choking on some crumbled cheese at a wine and cheese tasting event. They used to laugh how their first meeting involved him grabbing her from behind and helping her spit out a wad of cheese she'd ingested onto the face of a woman who had cut Samantha in line for the day's event.

She couldn't have thanked him enough, insisting he stay with her and her friends for the rest of the day. That night, he took her to a wonderful dinner at a new fondu restaurant and they'd been together ever since.

How Jason came to exist inside the Goat Man was beyond her. But she'd be damned if she wouldn't do whatever she could to find a way to get him out.

Furiously blinking lights appeared a few blocks away. Once the police got there, she knew they wouldn't hesitate to unload every weapon they had into the Goat Man.

"We have to go," she said, attempting to take his hand. The Goat Man's flesh was as hot as a pizza oven. "Ouch!"

Samantha blew on her burned fingertips.

The Goat Man turned around for a moment to watch the police cruisers approaching. "Go...now."

"What?"

"Go now."

She felt a pull on her shirt. "Come on, Sam. Let's do what it says," Tina said.

"Come with us," Samantha said.

The Goat Man's body seemed to expand, his eyes glowing redder.

"Go...now!"

The power behind his words nearly knocked her off her feet. She reached back for Tina and Lou. She could tell she was losing Jason. Whatever had him in its grip was pulling him away from her. What she couldn't be sure of was if he was telling her to leave because he couldn't control himself, or was he saving her from the inevitable confrontation with the police?

Samantha ran with Lou and Tina at her sides.

She kept looking over her shoulder.

The Goat Man turned his back on them. Tires squealed as the cruisers stopped a good dozen feet from the towering cryptid. Samantha flinched when she heard the first shot.

It was followed by countless more.

CHAPTER THIRTEEN

Chad felt something wrap around his ankle a split-second before he fell face down onto the wet ground. The dampness did nothing to soften the impact. He felt and heard his nose break.

"Ow! Fuck!"

More concerning than his broken nose was the fact that whatever had tripped him still had him in its grip.

He had to wipe his watering eyes clear to get a better look at it.

And then he wished he hadn't.

Something that resembled a person melded with a blob but with flesh straight from a barbecue pit held fast to his ankle. When it grimaced, too-white teeth gleamed through the crisped flesh. A pair of wide, staring eyes bore into his soul.

Chad screamed for all he was worth, even though he knew there wasn't anyone around to hear or help him. There was no shame in shrieking when an abomination had ahold of you.

"Get the hell off me!"

He kicked his leg, hoping to break free from its grip. The blackened fingers only tightened around his ankle, restricting the flow of blood.

Another hand flopped forward, just missing his free leg. Chad tried to find some kind of purchase in the grass, hoping for a sturdy tree root, to help pull him away from the burned person, if that in fact is what it was.

For someone who looked like they should be dead, how were they so strong?

His rushing blood thrummed in his ears. He kept kicking, to no avail.

Then, with a voice that sounded just as incinerated as its skin, the thing said, "Kiiiillll mmmmeeee."

Talking didn't make it any less horrifying. In fact, Chad's fear went into hyper drive.

How in the name of God could it talk?

And then it hit him.

God had nothing to do with this, or the raving Goat Man.

He had willingly entered the devil's playground, and now he was going to pay for being so stupid.

"Dooooo iiiiittttt."

This time, it was able to grab his other leg. It used his jeans to claw its way closer to his chest.

Nononononono! Chad thrashed about as if he were having a grand mal seizure.

"Kiiiiiillll mmmmeeeee."

That paper thin voice had breath that could melt an iron fence. Chad couldn't breathe. He worried he was about to have a heart attack, and then wondered if maybe that wasn't the best possible outcome for him right now.

The crispy creature had made it all the way up to his crotch. An image of it biting down on his cock left him lightheaded.

The tire iron!

Yes. In his panic, he'd forgotten all about the tire iron. He must have dropped it when he fell.

Chad struggled to sit up, his face just a foot away from the leering thing hovering over his crotch.

His hands felt around the grass. His nose throbbed. His vision was gauzy at best.

Fingertips went cold when they touched the steel of the tire iron. He snatched it up and held it high over his head, tempted to whip out some line Bruce Campbell would have uttered in the movies.

Instead, he settled for wordlessly thumping the monstrosity on the top of what he assumed was its head. The sound of a cracking eggshell preceded a hiss of steam as smoke shot out of the jagged wound in its skull.

The thing let loose with a banshee wail that made Chad's blood curdle.

It still tried to pull itself closer to his face, despite a head that was now split in two, both sides falling further and further apart.

"Get the fuck offa me!"

Chad swung the tire iron again, this time hitting it in what passed for shoulders. The blackened thing spun away, the stuff coming out of its head wound whistling like a tea kettle.

He jumped to his feet, flicking off any bits of the horror that still clung to his clothes.

It writhed on the damp ground, a bundle of nerves that refused to die. He approached it cautiously, the tire iron at the ready to finish what it had started.

"Whhhyyyy…..Mmmmaasssssterrrrr?"

Sweet Jesus, how was it still talking?

Hopping from one foot to the other, fighting the urge to run, Chad said, "I'm not your master."

A lone eye rolled in its ruined head, glaring at him.

Then it started to laugh.

Chad didn't know which was worse, the laughing or the screaming or the steam escaping its head.

When the laughter devolved into a throaty chuckle, the snickering of a killer moments before he snuffed out a life, Chad decided laughter was not the best medicine.

"Fffodddeeerrr fffor the mmmaaaasssterrrr."

"If any of us looks like fodder, it's you, buddy."

Why was he talking to it? Chad felt himself losing his grip on reality.

Because I came here to find answers. And even though this thing is straight from my worst nightmares, it can talk.

He stepped closer, but this time it didn't bother to reach for him. Making sure he kept a safe distance from it, he asked, "What are you? What happened out here?"

The eye, so white in the darkness, rolled in its socket before focusing on him again.

"Luuupitaaa."

"Lupita?"

He had a hard time believing this hunk of flesh had once been a woman. Or anything living, for that matter.

"Did you do this?"

"Iffff I aaanswerrrr, willll you killll meeee? Waaaant to beee with mmmmaaassterrrr."

Chad had a terrible feeling in the pit of his stomach who Lupita's master could be. Was he near? Chad's skin crawled.

He squatted so he could address Lupita eye to eye. "If your master is who I think he is, I'm not sure he wants you. I mean, look at you."

The eye swiveled, taking in its burned form.

"I don't think I could kill you if I tried. But I can make you worse." He lifted the tire iron. "So, let's talk."

CHAPTER FOURTEEN

Jason felt himself slipping away.

One second, he was staring at Samantha, wondering at the fear and confusion in her eyes, troubled by his own tangled thoughts and emotions.

Now, he felt like a backseat passenger in his own mind, watching as three police cruisers came to a halt, vomiting out six officers, all with guns drawn at him. The image wavered, a red tint forming over his eyes.

What was going on? Why did they look like they wanted to shoot him?

He heard a muted clap. And then another. And then many more.

They were shooting at him! And for some reason, he was just standing there. He couldn't feel anything. Was he dying? Surely they couldn't all miss him. He'd never handled a gun before – Jason was a pacifist in every sense of the word – but even he could hit his mark at this short distance.

Now the police were disappearing under a swirling mucous of crimson, and Jason felt himself tumbling down, down, down...

"You gotta be fucking with me!" Officer Tyndall fired off another round from his shotgun. Its chest should be bloody ribbons. He saw its flesh ripple, but nothing seemed to penetrate.

"Don't stop!" his partner, Seth Crisp, wailed above the crackle of gunfire. "We'll find a weak spot."

Tyndall wasn't so sure of that.

When they had spoken to eyewitnesses to the murder spree back at the taco place, he'd heard the name Goat Man uttered over and over again. The town's popular monster was good for the occasional tourist and for finding a way to get your girl to hold you tight when you took her to the bridge. It was not known for going on a rampage, turning the streets red.

He and Crisp had thought it might be some lunatic dressed up as the infamous beast. A lot of people all over were on the verge of snapping. The world's sanity was strung tighter than a stripper's thong, as his grandfather liked to say. This had to be a case of some closet nutter losing it altogether, going for a body count that would give him longstanding infamy.

He couldn't have foreseen how wrong they were.

This was no mental patient in a costume.

This was the goddamn Goat Man in the flesh, and there was a lot of – impenetrable – flesh to see. What the hell were they supposed to do when bullets didn't even make it flinch?

He racked his shotgun and fired again, this time aiming for the hairy legs, specifically the knee joint. Some hair fluttered, as if a breeze had blown by, but that was it.

The Goat Man leaned its head forward, bullets sending up sparks as they bounced off its mammoth curved horns.

"Hold fire! Hold fire! There's someone over there!"

Tyndall and Crisp looked to where Officer Kim Napolitano was pointing. Sure enough, there was a guy on the ground right next to the creature.

Fucking great, Tyndall thought. *Now we'll have to explain how and why we killed a civilian.*

Plenty of people had already been taken out by this abomination tonight. The last thing the terrified citizens needed to worry about was getting caught in the crossfire from the very men and women who were trying to protect them.

"Wait, he's moving," Crisp said. The man struggled to stand, and when he did, Tyndall's partner added, "What in the blue hell is wrong with him?"

"Is he covered in blood?"

There wasn't any crimson on his clothes. It was just his flesh. He looked like someone who had been eating nothing but beets for a year.

"I don't think so," Tyndall said.

"Well, his blood pressure must be sky high."

The police stood their ground and held their fire when the monster grabbed the red man by the back of his neck and lifted him high.

"Put him down!" Tyndall and Napolitano shouted in unison.

The beast did as it was told.

It launched the red man at them. His body slammed into the side of Tyndall and Crisp's cruiser, spine and ribs cracking on impact. The body split open along the side. Instead of blood, a strange, orange gas poured out of his body.

None of the police had time to react as the gas morphed into undulating fingers that probed deep into every mouth.

Tyndall went rigid as an iron bar as the strange vapor that smelled like rotten eggs invaded his body. It pushed down deep into his stomach, coiling through his intestinal tract, seeping into every organ until it seemed to find his very soul.

The officers, still on their feet, thrashed about as their bodies were taken over, one by one. Eyes rolled up, revealing red-veined whites, joints cracked and voices gurgled.

Tyndall's last thought, before he slipped into the blackness that clawed at his every atom, was a simple plea not to be dragged to hell.

Samantha refused to run anymore.

Jason was back there, or at least some part of him, and the police were using him as target practice. No amount of pleading or pulling on Tina and Lou's part could get her to move.

She watched as the police shot at the Goat Man – Jason – over and over again. Samantha cried out for her boyfriend, but her voice was drowned out in the cacophony of gunfire.

To her amazement, the creature that housed her boyfriend stood tall through it all, completely unphased.

"Bitch, we've got to go!" Tina said. "See, Jason's fine. Crap, it's weird calling that thing Jason."

"It is him, right?"

"If I didn't hear it with my own ears, I would have told you that you were off your nut. But it sure as hell sounded and talked like Jason."

"If it wasn't him, he would have killed us," Samantha said. That was twice now they'd been able to walk away from the Goat Man, where everyone else had been slaughtered. "We need to help him."

"Help him?" Tina cried. "How? He's destroying everything and everyone he sees and he's indestructible. What can we possibly do?"

"Uh, guys," Lou said.

They followed her gaze and watched as the Goat Man launched the red man that had been chasing Lou at the police. He broke open like a tear gas canister, except this gas moved as if it were alive, making a bee line for the police. Seconds later, they were doing a kind of Saint Vitus dance in the street while croaking out a chorus of pain.

As one, they flopped onto the pavement, continuing to twist and contort their bodies in ways that seemed impossible. Bones and joints must have been dislocating to get them to move that way.

Samantha had a feeling she knew what they were looking at. She had seen her share of videos going down rabbit holes online when she couldn't shut her brain down after a long day. A simple search for a coconut cookie recipe sliding, somehow, into videos on real life exorcisms.

"I think they're possessed," she said, her heart beating in her throat.

"Well, we're not sticking around to find out for sure," Tina said, latching onto Samantha's wrist. "If your boyfriend can now put demons in people, we're outta here."

Samantha was dragged around the corner, putting the Goat Man behind them.

Tina picked up a metal garbage can, dumped the refuse on the ground, and used it to smash the window of the nearest car. She opened the door and shoved Lou and Samantha inside, then slid under the steering wheel to hotwire the car. It didn't take her long to get the engine started. She had the car barreling down the street seconds later.

When Samantha grabbed the wheel, the car scraped against a parked SUV, sending up a fireworks display of sparks.

"What the hell are you doing?" Tina blurted, punching Samantha in the arm.

"I told you, we have to help Jason."

"And again, how?"

Lou stayed silent in the back seat, looking out the window with ping pong ball eyes.

"I don't know. But we can't keep running away. You've seen how well that plan has gone. My boyfriend is back there, and he needs us."

"Sam, your boyfriend is now a giant, maniac monster. Why don't you sit tight and Google how to fix him? I'll bet it'll be the first search in Google history with zero results."

Samantha, normally the quiet one, the one who let Tina do all the tough talking and walking, punched Tina back. "I said stop!"

Tina looked at her as if she'd lost her sanity. And perhaps they all had.

"Sam, chill."

"Stop the car."

"No."

Lou watched them argue as the car went through a red light. She saw a car coming toward them at the next intersection.

"Watch out!" Lou barked.

She was too late.

CHAPTER FIFTEEN

The Goat Man looked at the pinkening horizon, then at the twitching minions at its feet.

More shrieking sirens were headed its way.

It was time to go. Its lust for blood and carnage had been sated...for the moment. The devilish beast ripped a manhole cover from the street and flung it aside with enough power to bury it in the brickwork of a building across the street.

With a single look, the Goat Man commanded the fallen police officers to slide along the pavement like eels until they dropped into the open manhole. They splashed into the darkness below.

Before joining them, the Goat Man took one long, last look down the empty street.

It felt as if it should be looking for something. Something very specific. A tiny bubble of a foreign emotion swelled in its massive chest, and quickly died.

The hole wasn't large enough to accommodate its mass, so it kicked at the blacktop with its hooves until it had widened the circle. The Goat Man jumped into the sewer, savoring the gloom and foul odors. It stepped through the sea of filthy minions, having to stoop to keep its horns from shredding the ceiling, and powered through the labyrinth.

Chad slammed both feet on the brakes and cut the wheel hard. His car spun in a tight circle. He was sure he was about to flip over.

Eyes closed, hands in a death grip on the wheel, Chad gritted his teeth and waited for the sound of crunching metal.

His head whipped sharply to the side, and he miraculously found himself in one piece and not covered in glass or with the steering wheel embedded in his chest. It was only once the car had stopped that the air bags deployed. The blast nearly knocked him unconscious. The pain in his skull was excruciating. For a terrifying moment, he thought he couldn't breathe.

Hands pounding on the airbag, he struggled to wiggle out from under its oppressive weight.

To his great relief, it quickly deflated. He took a deep, wet breath, and saw the blood on the surface of the airbag, which was now looking more like a used condom.

The taste of copper flooded his mouth. It was all he could smell. His nose was clogged.

Chad touched his nose.

Was it possible to break an already broken nose? Fear and adrenaline had done a great job at masking the pain until now. He spat out a gob of blood and breathed through his mouth.

After collecting himself for a bit and fighting through the pain and tears in his eyes, he looked into the back seat.

Well, it looks the same.

"Are you okay?"

He turned to the voice and couldn't believe his eyes.

"Samantha?"

"Chad?"

"Can you help me out?"

"Yeah, sure."

Samantha gingerly assisted him as he crawled out of the car. His neck made a startling cracking noise, instantly followed by a flood of agony. Had to be whiplash.

"Jesus, I can't get rid of you."

He was flabbergasted to see Lou with Samantha and Tina.

"What are the odds?" he muttered. Seriously, what were they? It made him think something bigger than all of them was in play here.

"Has it been your goal all night to kill us?" Tina said.

Pinching the bridge of his nose and spitting out gobs of blood, Chad said, "I wasn't the one driving like a maniac. If I didn't get out of the way, we'd be chop meat in two tin cans."

Tina went to say something, but was stopped by a harsh look from Samantha.

"We have to get out of here," Samantha said. "Why don't you come with us?"

Chad looked up and down the street. Dawn was upon them, which would make it easier to spot the Goat Man if it were barreling their way. "Where's the Goat Man?"

Samantha clutched his arm. "We'll tell you later. Come on."

"Wait." Chad wrestled away from her grip. "I have, um, something that has to come with us."

"We're not letting you film us for your stupid show," Lou said.

"No, nothing like that." Though he wished Michael was here to do just that. For all the horror of this night, if they had captured it on film, they would have been set for life.

Chad stumbled to his car and opened the back door. The girls stood behind him.

"What the fuck is that?" Tina said. "Looks like a burnt lump of the biggest brisket ever crammed in a smoker."

The lump of brisket shuddered at the sound of Tina's voice. A pair of arms separated from the charred mass, followed by a misshapen head. Tina barked a slew of profanities while Samantha and Lou gasped.

"*That* is Lupita. And if we're going to figure this out, she's the key."

Lupita's eye opened and Lou yelped.

"How the...I mean, what the..." Samantha stammered.

"Exactly," Chad said. "If we can find someplace safe, Lupita might be able to help us."

Tina refused to let Chad put the barbecued lump of whatever Lupita was in the car with them. The trunk was just fine.

They drove to Lou's house because she said her parents would be freaked out. The Goat Man's murder spree was all over the news on the radio and Internet. While Tina drove, her passengers were glued to their phones, babbling headlines. None of the official news agencies were calling the night's devastation an act of their local cryptid gone insane, but there were posts on social media from people who had been in its murderous path, some with blurry pictures. So far, it seemed like most people not only didn't believe the posts, but were angry as hell at the posters for 'making light' of a tragedy.

Chad and Lou also exchanged what each had been through since they'd separated. Tina kept quiet, eyes on the road, waiting for the Goat Man to magically reappear.

"Where's their car?" Lou said as they pulled into her driveway.

She bolted out of the car and ran to the back of the house.

"Maybe I should go inside with her," Samantha said.

Tina kept the engine idling, listening out for any signs of Lupita rumbling around the trunk. It made her skin crawl just thinking about it. "Give her a few minutes. Her parents might not be happy with a total stranger barging into their house."

They sat quietly for a short while, until Lou came out the front door in tears. "They're not here." Her mascara ran down her face in dark rivers. "They went out for dinner and a movie in town last night. Do you think…"

She broke down. Samantha popped out of the car and held her while she sobbed.

"Damn, I feel bad for the kid," Chad said. "She lost her boyfriend and parents all in the same night."

"Yeah, it sucks. A lot of people lost someone they loved last night."

"Makes you wonder how we got through it all."

It looked like Samantha was holding Lou up. The girl clung to her like a life raft.

Tina turned around to face Chad. He looked like hell. She was sure she didn't look much better at the moment. "You think God has a plan for us?" She rolled her eyes just in case he didn't get her sarcasm.

"Don't be so quick to dismiss the idea. According to Lupita, they were making a sacrifice to the Goat Man as a way to gain favor with the devil."

Tina felt her temper ignite. "Oh, so now we're relying on that lump of shit in the trunk for information? Give me a break."

"That lump of shit is just as strange as a maniacal Goat Man ravaging the city. But we've seen them both and we know they're for real."

Tina spun around. "Whatever. Just don't get all Jesus freak on us. I don't have time for that shit."

"Hey, the last time I was in church was for my Confirmation. My parents gave up after that and I had zero interest. What I am saying is that there are opposing sides to everything. Darkness and light. Good and evil. And this Goat Man is most definitely evil. For some reason, we're all still alive and, despite our running all over the place, we keep smacking into each other. Coincidence?"

"Could just mean you're a stalker."

"Don't flatter yourself. You're not my type."

"Thank God for that."

Chad's face lit up. "See. God is everywhere."

"Please just shut up."

"I'm just saying."

"Well, here's something you can ask Lupita. Is the Goat Man really Samantha's boyfriend?"

Chad cocked his head, scratched at the side of his broken nose and winced. "What?"

"Oh yeah. Somehow, some way, it appears that Jason is the Goat Man, or a part of him, or whatever. You think a benevolent God would allow that to happen?"

"Holy shit."

"More like unholy shit."

The back passenger door opened and Samantha helped Lou get inside. She was still sniffling but seemed to be more under control. When Samantha sidled up next to Tina, she said, "I think it's best she stays with us for now."

"Shouldn't she be home if the cops show up with news about, you know?" Tina said.

Samantha scolded her for her insensitivity with a look. "After last night, I'm not sure if there are any cops left. It's going to take at least a week for the city to recover."

"That's only if the Goat Man goes away," Chad piped up from the back seat. "If he doesn't, they'll have to call in the military."

Tina watched Samantha go pale. The death of the Goat Man would mean the death of Jason. Right? Tina wasn't sure, but it seemed to be a safe assumption.

"So now what do we do?" Tina said.

"We can go to my place and regroup," Samantha replied. She checked her phone, scrolling from screen to screen. "It looks like the Goat Man has stopped. For now. I feel like I'm going to pass out. We can crash for a little bit and figure out what to do later."

"What about Lupita?" Chad asked.

"That disgusting thing stays in the trunk. If you don't want it to feel lonely, you can crawl right in with it," Tina said.

Chad settled into his seat, visibly nauseated by the thought. "Works for me."

Tina backed out of the driveway. "If I had my way, we'd dump that thing in the trash and drive until the wheels fall off."

No one responded.

Tina wouldn't insist on getting her way this time. Samantha needed her, and Sam was not going anywhere until she figured out how to get Jason back. Tina doubted it was even possible, but she was willing to try. Samantha made them impervious to the Goat Man last night.

She hoped it stayed that way.

CHAPTER SIXTEEN

Samantha set Lou up on the couch. The teen was asleep by the time she draped a blanket over her.

Chad collapsed in a chair by the TV with a bottle of water in his hand. He took a sip and thanked her. She'd given him cotton balls that were now stuffed in his nostrils, the ends more red than white.

"I have stronger stuff than water," she whispered so as not to wake Lou.

"I'd take high test moonshine at this point."

She found the bottle of Knob Creek in the kitchen. She had only used it in the past to make bourbon cupcakes and muffins. Not today. She poured three healthy glasses and doled them out. Tina knocked hers back as if it were a shot without so much as a grimace. Chad's hand shook a bit as he took a sip. Samantha drank from her glass, feeling as if her insides were on fire.

"Lightweight," Tina said jokingly.

Samantha put her glass down. "And proud of it. I'm going to bed."

Tina finished Samantha's bourbon. "I'm right behind you."

Chad's eyelids were at half-mast. "I'll finish this and take a quick nap."

Samantha and Tina went to the bedroom and kicked off their shoes, collapsing onto the bed. On the bedside table was a framed picture of Samantha and Jason holding each other on the beach. They were tan and happy and had the world by the balls.

There was no stopping the silent tears that fell. "Why Jason?"

Tina snuggled closer and put her arms around her. "I don't know. But we're going to do whatever we can to get him back. Even if it means talking to that thing outside. Okay?"

Sam sniffed and nodded.

Sleep came quickly.

Guided by instinct, the Goat Man led his possessed minions to the sewer opening nearest the path to the woods. It punched its way through the manhole cover and too-tight opening, the minions shambling their way up the ladder and following it like zombies, their bodies jerking and twitching, mouths foaming with vomit, throats tremoring with guttural noises.

The cryptid stepped onto the bridge named after it and paused, taking in the dead man. It vaguely recalled pummeling the man earlier in the night. The sight of the pulverized corpse gave it a tremor of satisfaction.

Hooves clacking over the wooden planks, the Goat Man headed back into the woods, avoiding the clearing where it had been birthed. It needed to remain hidden for a while to collect its strength. There was so much more to be done.

A beast from hell couldn't simply exist on the infernal rage that writhed within it.

No, the Goat Man needed sustenance after a long, brutal night of death and ruination.

It settled down against a tree, the heat from its flesh baking the bark, turning it black. Its seven minions flopped to the ground, staring at it with just the whites of their eyes. When the Goat Man uttered a sharp and violent bleat, the minion closest to it wriggled along the ground until it was close enough for the creature to grab it by the top of its head. It pulled the possessed policeman close enough so it could pull his head back, exposing his neck. The Goat Man dove into the tender flesh, chewing into his trachea and crunching on his thyroid cartilage. Blood and vomit bathed the Goat Man's bristly fur.

When it had eaten clear to the spine, it reached into the hole, rummaging around until it clamped its fingers on his heart. It pulled the heart free and swallowed it whole.

Casting the body aside, it called out for the next, repeating the process until there was a pile of leaking bodies at its side.

Belly full, the Goat Man closed its eyes and rested.

And in the silence, for no animals or insects would come near, it heard a voice, as if from deep within itself, crying to get out.

Chad awoke to the smell of coffee. One eye open, he spotted Tina in the kitchen pouring herself a cup. He checked his phone and saw that two hours had passed. He felt as if he needed about another twenty to feel human again.

"Any coffee to spare?" he asked as he wiped the sleep from his eyes.

"Didn't mean to wake you," Tina said. "I can't sleep more than a couple of hours at a time. Prison fucks up your sleep cycle. I bet you like it light and sweet."

His bones cracked as he got out of the chair. "You'd lose that bet. Black with one sugar, please."

He joined her in the kitchen as they drank their coffee in silence, stealing glances at Lou who was curled into the fetal position on the couch. When they weren't looking at the teen, they were checking their phones. It appeared the murder spree had not resumed since they'd crashed at

Samantha's. What the news reported and what people on social media reported were polar opposites of one another.

"Are they willfully this ignorant?" Chad said, showing the CNN report to Tina. "I mean, there are tons of pictures and videos everywhere of the fucking thing."

"Yeah, but have you noticed they are all hazy?"

Tina scrolled through a slew of pictures on Instagram. It wasn't like all the blurry pictures of bigfoot and the Loch Ness monster. Everything around the Goat Man was in focus. But the beast itself appeared to be encased in a kind of rippling mist.

"Looks like the way heat rises from scorching blacktop," Chad said.

"Kinda makes sense. I mean, if that creepy thing you have in the trunk is right, the Goat Man is from hell, or someplace close to it, like Detroit." She grinned, and Chad couldn't help smiling.

"My parents are from Detroit," he said. "My dad worked in the Ford factory, at least until he got a better job in Lansing."

"Michigan. Yeah, that fits you."

"What does that mean?"

They were interrupted when Lou sat up gasping. "My parents!"

She fumbled around the blanket until she found her phone. She tapped the screen and put the phone to her ear. The despondent look on her face told Chad and Tina that they hadn't answered.

"Don't freak out just yet," Tina said. "They could be detained by the cops giving their statement if they were near one of the Goat Man's rampages."

"But they'd have their phone. They'd answer their phone!"

Chad hustled into the living room and sat beside her. "It's been, what, over twelve hours since they left?"

Lou nodded.

"Their charge could have run out by now. Just take a deep breath. You want something to drink?"

Lou picked at her cuticles. "You have Red Bull?"

Chad looked over at Tina. "Sam hates that stuff. Coffee, apple juice, or water?"

"Coffee, I guess. With a lot of milk and six sugars."

Tina prepared her caffeine and sugar bomb while Chad wrapped the blanket around her. Lou's eyes were glassy, staring at the wall, but Chad knew she was looking deep within herself, perhaps at memories of her parents. That would be better than relaying the horror she'd lived through over the past night.

Tina had started cracking eggs when Samantha came bursting out of her bedroom, phone in hand. "Have you seen this?"

"Seen what?" Tina asked. "The news lying about what happened last night? Nothing new there."

Samantha shoved her phone in Tina's face. "There are all kinds of calls to form a posse today to find the Goat Man and kill it. Look."

Chad went to the kitchen to stand over Tina's shoulder. Lou remained on the couch, sipping her coffee, not even acknowledging Samantha's presence.

"Holy crap, Texas justice is really a thing," Chad said. Samantha scrolled through all of the various messages on several platforms with people calling to gather at the Whataburger parking lot at five o'clock. There was an alarming number of positive responses, some of them sharing pics of themselves holding their guns. These people were angry because they had lost someone and their city had been wrecked. For a brief moment, Chad almost felt bad for the Goat Man. "Some of those guns look a lot bigger and more powerful than anything the police had last night."

"They're gonna blow that thing to shit," Tina said, setting the bowl of eggs aside.

Samantha slammed the phone facedown on the counter. "Not just *that thing*. Jason!"

"Now that I've had a chance to think about it, I'm not so sure that's Jason. We saw what it could do with that dude that went after Lou and those cops. Who knows what kind of other powers it has? It could have been mimicking Jason."

"So how did it know Jason's nickname for me?"

"Maybe it ate him," Lou said from the couch. "You know, absorbed his memories and stuff."

"You're not helping. Drink your coffee, kid," Tina said.

"And why didn't it kill us – both times – when it could have easily pulled us apart?"

Tina shook her head. "I don't know, Sam. You could be right and that is Jason. But now, in the light of day, I'm having doubts."

Samantha turned to Chad. "Take me to that...whatever...in the trunk."

"You have the keys?" Chad asked Tina.

"If it was my car, I would. My question is, should we eat before we have to look at it?"

Samantha stormed out of the apartment with Chad and Tina hurrying up behind her. Lou didn't get off the couch.

Before popping the trunk open, Tina looked up and down the street. "We're clear. Don't want anyone to walk by and catch a glimpse of dark and crispy in there."

The trunk opened a crack. The stench that assaulted their noses and senses had them all dry heaving.

Chad turned away, his eyes watering. "Holy cow. It must have died overnight." That would be a shame. He'd risked his life finding Lupita and his sanity just touching the mound of burned flesh to get it in his car.

"Did it really qualify as alive last night?" Tina asked before retching.

Samantha was the one bravest enough to open the trunk all the way. She pinched her nose as she stared at the abomination. "Wake up."

Chad peeked into the trunk. The arms had retracted. It looked like a sick elephant had taken a dump inside it. Vomit exploded from his mouth and nose before he could even attempt to swallow it back. Yellowish chunks landed on the mangled body.

Lupita's eye flashed open. So did her mouth as she wailed in disgust.

CHAPTER SEVENTEEN

Lou tried calling her mother and father again. Each time, it went to voicemail. She texted them to call her, but didn't expect a reply.

I'm an orphan.

Did they put seventeen-year-old orphans in group homes, or would she be allowed to get her own place? Both sets of her grandparents were dead and her mother had a brother who had gone off to Asia to 'find himself' years ago. Uncle Jay was a self-absorbed schmuck. There was no way she'd live with him if they managed to find his new age ass.

It would take a while for the system to realize she was alone in the world. Everything would be flooded in the aftermath of what the Goat Man had done last night. She would live in the house as long as she could, until the bills piled up and the bank came to take it.

One thing she wasn't going to do was go to school. She could see the principal, teachers and guidance counselors coming up with their lame ways to help the students cope. They'd just make things worse with their tributes, vigils and grief counseling.

Lou felt guilty for last night and that she deserved her grief.

If she hadn't dragged Henry out there because she wanted a little excitement with her sex, maybe the Goat Man would have kept to the woods. Instead, it had killed Henry and chased after her, and she'd led it straight to the city. Her city.

She knew she should be crying, but she felt so empty. She drank her coffee and wondered what she was going to do next.

"Fffffuuuucck youuuuuu," Lupita snarled.

With the trunk wide open, the offensive funk that was Lupita had dissipated. Chad's vomit did nothing to improve her appearance. Samantha had no idea how a person could look like that and still be alive, but she was past wondering how anything happened. She just needed answers.

"Chad said you and your dumbass friends were performing a Satanic ritual in the woods. Is that right?"

The eye rolled to her. "Willll youuuu killl mmmmeeee?"

Samantha snarled. "With pleasure. Now, tell me what happened."

The onyx flesh quivered as Lupita shifted slightly. Chad's vomit dripped into the folds of her barbecued skin. Tina and Chad kept looking away, but Samantha was laser focused.

"Callled our mmmaasssssterrrr," Lupita said. "Buuuut we dissssspleassssed himmmm. The saaaaacrificcce wassss ruinnnnned."

"What were you sacrificing?" Or should she have asked who? Idiots did their little Satan crap out there all the time because of the Goat Man legend.

But this Lupita had been the real deal. She had done something the others hadn't.

An awful smile stretched across the crackling flesh. "What elsssse? A goaaaat forrr the Goooat Mannnn."

That made an awful kind of sense. "So, what ruined it?"

The smile disappeared. "That maaaannnn. Cammmme at the heiiight of rrrritualll. Lighninnnng sssstruck. I...I wentttt to helllll. Buuuut mmmmasterrrr sssent me baaaack."

A man walked into their ritual?

"What did the man look like?"

The eye closed. "Youuuu killll mmmmeeee nnnow?"

"No, but maybe I'll have Chad upchuck on you again."

Lupita's eye rolled around like a loose marble, which was probably the closest she could come to giving an expression of disgust.

"Taaallllll. Beaaaarrrrrd. Ssssstupid."

"Sounds like Jason," Tina quipped.

"Cut it out," Samantha snapped back.

Jason was tall and he did have a beard. He was far from stupid.

Samantha gasped, stepping away from the trunk.

"What's wrong?" Tina asked. "I mean, aside from everything lately."

"The cats. The last time I talked to him, he was so upset about the cats."

"What cats?" Chad asked.

Samantha paced around the rear of the car. "We were on the phone, and he was watching the news. He stopped when there was a report about a litter of kittens being found left in plastic bags out in the woods behind the Goat Man's Bridge. It made him so mad, he started yelling. Not at me, just shouting in general about how fucked up people are. He said they should post police in the woods and arrest anyone who they found with an animal because of all the, you know, idiots like her." She jerked her thumb at Lupita. "I'll bet he went out there on his own to catch someone in the act. I mean, he really loves cats. Crap, I should stop at his place to feed them."

Tina massaged her temples. "Well, sounds like mission accomplished for Jason. Except he became a goat instead of saving it." She stopped and snickered, trying to hide her smile. Samantha looked stricken. "I'm sorry. It's just so ridiculous sounding, it's funny."

"No," Samantha said. "Not really."

Chad joined Samantha's pacing. "So, your boyfriend goes out there to save some animals and gets caught in a kind of Satanic crossfire. He merged with the goat and now is maybe possessed by the devil or some other kind of demon. None of it makes sense, but it's the best we've got."

Samantha covered her face when the tears started. "And if we don't find a way to save him by five o'clock, the town is going to kill him."

Chad snapped his fingers. "Who do possessed people turn to?"

"Huh?" Tina said.

"A priest! We need to find a priest who can come with us and find your boyfriend and…and exorcise him."

Wiping away her tears, Samantha said, "If we told a priest our story, he'd think we were either punking him or out of our minds. Even if he saw the pictures and videos that are out there."

With narrowing eyes, Tina said, "Yeah, a regular priest would. But I know we could convince Father Farmer to do what we asked."

"Father Farmer? He's an old man. If he looked at the Goat Man, he'd have a stroke," Samantha said.

"He's stronger than he looks. I once spotted him doing a little power walk out by the park one night. And I heard from Mack, you know, the bartender at Sully's, that he goes there a lot for some day drinking. Mack said he could drink just about anyone under the table."

"Oh great. An old alcoholic priest is just what we need," Chad said.

"He's the best chance we have. Jesus, I can't believe I'm saying that." She checked her phone. "We're burning daylight. Chad, go grab Lou and let's hit the road."

She slammed the trunk. There were muffled thumps as Lupita banged on the lid, along with another plea to 'kiilllll meeeee'.

"We will when we're good and ready!" Tina shouted at the closed trunk.

Chad ran back into the building.

"Do you really think he'll do it?" Samantha said.

"The dude likes me. A lot. He will."

Samantha hugged herself even though the day had started out warm. "I hope you're right, because we don't have time for you to be wrong."

Tina put her arm around Samantha's shoulder. "I'm your ride or die, bitch, and we're going to get Jason back."

Chad returned two minutes later, trying to catch his breath. "Lou's gone."

Samantha knew they should probably try to find her, but that would waste the one thing they didn't have in large supply – time.

"Maybe she went back to her house," Tina said. "She's better off on her own instead of joining our potential suicide mission. Don't worry about it."

They piled into the car, but Samantha couldn't help herself from worrying.

While the Goat Man slept, the leaves on the tree turned black and fell like grimy snowflakes around it. The grass browned and shriveled back into the soil. A passing cardinal swooped too close and fell out of the air, dead before it hit the ground.

All around the Goat Man, nature withered and died. The growing penumbra of decay resembled a blast zone, where nothing had survived, besides the great slumbering beast, waves of heat curling off its body.

Deep within the Goat Man, a tiny voice shouted to be heard, to claw its way from the twisting depths of nothingness.

CHAPTER EIGHTEEN

Lou couldn't believe someone was crazy enough to turn their Uber app on, but was grateful for the ride back to her house. She rushed out of Samantha's apartment, purposefully avoiding them.

Samantha was convinced that her boyfriend was somehow part of the Goat Man and determined to save him.

The last thing Lou wanted to do was save that wild monster.

There was no way she could stop it on her own. But the growing posse pledging to find it and kill it would do just fine.

And Lou was going to be a part of it.

She stepped into her house and was immediately struck by the silence. It was more than just the quiet. It felt empty, abandoned. All their stuff was there, but the life of the home was gone and wouldn't be coming back.

At this time of the morning, the television would be on tuned to the news. Her mother would be cooking in the kitchen, making Lou breakfast before school, packing a lunch for herself and Lou's father, all while putting on her makeup and getting ready for work at the real estate office. The shower upstairs would be running, her father's radio blasting some talk show, usually something about sports.

The silence of the house brought tears to her eyes.

Something bumped against her leg, startling her. Her cat, Drusilla, purred and looked up at her with her hungry face. Lou picked the cat up and buried her face in its fur.

"I'm so sorry I didn't feed you when I stopped by last night. I'll give you two cans to make up for it."

She set the bowl on the kitchen table, something her mother would totally freak out over if she were here. Watching Drusilla attack her food, Lou wished with all of her being that her mother would walk into the kitchen and pitch a fit.

Lou had been such a shit to her parents lately. Typical teenage rebellion stuff, which in hindsight was pretty ridiculous, considering she'd be going to college next year. She wished she could take back all the fights, all the lies, just about everything she'd done the past couple of years.

Tears ran down her face as she walked up to her parents' bedroom. The smell of her mother's favorite perfume was still in the air. She went into their closet and found the metal box where her father kept his gun. When she was young, it used to be locked and up on a higher shelf.

The lid gave a slight squeak as it opened. The silver Ruger had a walnut grip and shined when the sun hit it just right. It was pretty big and very heavy, at least for Lou. Her father had taken her to the firing range one time, just a few months ago, as a way to find some way to bond with his recalcitrant daughter. She'd been shocked by how powerful and loud it had been.

Would it be enough to stop the Goat Man? Probably not. But she wouldn't be the only one out there ready to bring it down. Even bulletproof glass had a breaking point.

For just a moment, she considered taking her mother's .22, but decided against it. If the Ruger didn't work, the .22 would be less than worthless.

She set the Ruger on the kitchen counter and poured herself a bowl of cereal. While she crunched away at the multi-colored sugar bombs, she followed all of the posts about tonight's posse, the dark cloud of revenge above her roiling with each passing second.

Tina pulled the stolen car into the church's parking lot after their quick pitstop at Jason's, No surprise that he wasn't home. Samantha fed all of his cats and cleaned out the litter boxes. Tina wondered what Sam would do with all those cats if Jason never returned.

The eight o'clock weekday mass was just letting out. A few old ladies and one geezer in a cowboy hat straggled out, squinting into the sun. They were followed by a couple of dozen other people, which was not the norm. People must have been watching the news and needed some comfort.

Chad strode toward the church steps.

"He's not in there," Tina said. "We have to go to the rectory."

He paused, looking at the church, then at Tina.

"What, you thinking of going inside and lighting a candle or something?"

"I mean, it couldn't hurt."

Tina gave an exasperated sigh. "We don't have time."

Samantha grasped her hand as they headed for the rectory, Chad hurrying to catch up to them. The middle-aged woman who ran the day to day stuff at the rectory didn't look pleased to see them. Tina was not her favorite person in the world. So much for Christian kindness.

"Can I help you?" she asked with barely veiled suspicion. There were dark circles under her eyes.

"Yes. We wanted to see Father Farmer."

The woman looked at Tina's empty hands. "It doesn't look like you're here to bring his meal."

"Nothing gets by you."

Samantha nudged Tina's side with her elbow.

"Sorry. We just wanted to ask him some questions."

Her eyes flicked from one to the other, and then she said, "He's indisposed right now. If you want, you can write down your questions and I'll give them to him."

Tina scowled. "What if I had something to confess? You think I'd write that down so you can get your jollies reading it?"

The woman's face hardened. "If it's confession you need, there are certain times to do so, in the confessional."

There was a slight commotion in the room behind her. Father Farmer popped into view, his hands in the air. "Dammit. I'd rather have a never-ending hemorrhoid than this arthritis." Books were scattered about his feet.

Tina slipped around the woman's desk and knelt down to pick them up, despite her protestations.

"Tina?" Father Farmer said. "What are you doing here at this hour?"

Samantha and Chad stood in the doorway.

"Do you mind if we talk for just a second?" Tina asked.

The woman angled out from behind her desk with her hands planted on her hips. "I tried to get them to just leave a message, Father."

He waved her off. "It's fine, it's fine." To Tina, he said, "Ah, I see you brought your friend. Samantha, right? And who is the patient? You see a doctor about that nose?"

"That's just Chad," Tina said, his books tucked under her arm. "Is there someplace private we can talk?" She cast a glance at the secretary.

"Sure, sure. Let's go to the kitchen."

They followed the priest as he shuffled into the bright kitchen and shut the folding doors behind him. "I was coming down for some coffee. Would you like some?"

"Here, let me make it for you," Samantha said. There was an old percolator on the stovetop. He pointed out where to find the can of coffee and she got to work.

They sat around the round table and Father Farmer said, "So, what brings you here at what I'm sure is an ungodly hour for you? I'm sure last night's tragedy has you rattled. Chad, it looks like you were in the thick of things."

Tina clasped her hands together and leaned forward. "We were all in the thick of it. Thicker than any of us would have liked."

His face paled. "I guess the bright side is you're all here today. Thank the Lord. So many dead or wounded. Father Mark is at the hospital now. I was thinking of going over to help him."

"If you want to help, there's something else you can do," Tina said.

"Oh?"

Over the next ten minutes, Tina, Samantha and Chad told him everything that had happened the night before. He listened with growing confusion.

When they were done, he said, "So you want me to perform an exorcism on a goat creature because you think your boyfriend is somehow trapped within it?"

Tina pulled up some of the better pictures on her phone that were being shared on social media. Father Farmer took the phone from her and brought it so close to his face, the tip of his nose practically touched the screen. "Hard to tell what that is."

Samantha started to cry. "You have to believe us."

He gave the phone back to Tina. "That's a pretty wild assumption."

Tina felt the whole thing slipping away. It was time to take drastic action. She tugged her shirt down until her cleavage was bared. "You can see more of that if you agree to help us."

Father Farmer quickly looked away. "Stop embarrassing yourself, Tina. Put those things away."

Her cheeks burned as she lifted her shirt, taking note that Chad had enjoyed the peek. "But I thought..."

"That all priests are closet perverts," Father Farmer said. "It's not your fault. There is a minority of priests who have made it very easy for the media and public to paint us all with the same brush. Trust me, I have no desire to see you that way."

"I just thought, with the way you looked at me." It had been a long time since Tina had been rocked back on her heels like this. And by a priest, no less!

"Yes, you're a pretty girl, in a diamond in the rough sort of way. Look, I'm old, and when you get older, you appreciate youth more than you ever had when you were young yourself. I enjoy having you around because you remind me of better times."

"We have proof," Samantha said, saving Tina from further embarrassment.

The priest was intrigued. "Do you have this, ah, Goat Man, in your possession?"

Chad grinned. "Possession is exactly what we have to show you."

Father Farmer followed them to the car.

"You might want to step back while it airs out a bit," Tina warned him before she popped the trunk. The smell was atrocious. Father Farmer blanched.

"Please don't tell me you've killed someone," he said.

Tina looked inside. "Well, she's dead, sorta, but sorta not. And no, we had nothing to do with it."

The old man took a few faltering steps toward the open trunk. "You all know I'll have to call the police, right?" When he saw Lupita, and Lupita stared back at him, he made a quick sign of the cross and covered his mouth. "What in the name of heaven?"

"More like hell," Chad said.

"Father Farmer, this is Lupita," Tina said.

"Baaaack awaaaayyyy, Priesssssssst."

"It talks!"

Samantha grabbed his arm because he looked like he was about to fall.

"*It* was a woman who led a Satanic cult that got a little too close to the guy downstairs."

"This…this is impossible."

"It is, but it isn't, as you can see. And smell." Tina slammed the lid shut. "Now, will you help us?"

CHAPTER NINETEEN

The timetable to smoke out and bring the Goat Man to justice was moved up to noon. Many of the people who had promised to be there decided they could mourn their losses after the Goat Man was eradicated.

Lou drove her mother's car to the Whataburger lot. It was crammed with so many cars and people, she had to park two blocks away. The crowd was tightly packed together under a blue sky. A small podium had been set on an impromptu stage. Everyone was carrying a weapon. Some held rifles and shotguns. Others had their pistols tucked in holsters. She spotted a few guys with crossbows and a black woman with a sword.

Definitely watched too much Walking Dead, Lou thought. She'd seen what the Goat Man could do. Crossbows and swords weren't going to be worth a damn.

A man wearing a Dallas Cowboys t-shirt was at the podium, speaking through a bullhorn. Lou had to hop in order to see him over the taller men in front of her.

"It doesn't matter what they're reporting. We all know what we saw last night. It was a demon straight from hell!"

A few arms rose up, clutching Bibles. There were a lot of shouted 'amens' and various prayers were uttered. Lou went to church every Sunday because that's what her family always did. She didn't care much for it. In fact, she spent a lot of that time looking at all the hot guys in the pews around her.

"If you didn't lose someone close to you last night, I'm sure you know someone who has. There isn't a morgue big enough to handle what's been done to our city. A night like that will forever change us, and I fear not for the better.

But I can promise you one thing. What happened last night will not happen again!"

Everyone clapped, including Lou, riding the building wave of revenge-fueled euphoria. Her father's gun was heavy in her jacket pocket as it slapped against her side.

"There's no waiting around for the authorities to help us. This is our city. We're going to find that demon and send it right back to hell!"

The crowd roared, weapons held high.

"We're going to break out into various search parties with a team leader for each. The team leaders will keep in touch with each other. Once we find the demon, we'll make the chain of calls to get everyone at the beast's location and do to it what it has done to us!"

The response was deafening. Lou knew she should have been afraid, but all she could feel right now was excited at the prospect of getting back at the thing that had taken her parents and boyfriend away from her.

"We have word that it may have taken to the sewers, so we're gonna search for the son of a bitch above and below ground. Now, these men here wearing blue hats will be your team leaders. They'll divide you all into groups. But before that happens, let's take a moment to pray, not just for our success, but for the souls of all those taken by the demon."

An older woman came to the podium, cleared her throat, and started reading from the Bible. Lou put her hand in her pocket, running her fingers along the cold steel, anxious to get to the amen.

Samantha sat in the back with Chad. Father Farmer sat up front with Tina. Before they'd hit the road, he'd gone back to his room to collect some things, returning with a battered black briefcase. His cheeks were flushed and he wore a steady 'what the hell am I doing?' expression.

As they drove across town, they passed by scene after scene of carnage. Cars were smashed, bodies lay under bloody sheets. Samantha took note that all of the police on the scene were state police, not local. She also saw some cars bearing logos from surrounding towns and cities.

The discussion on where to go had been brief. Samantha couldn't see the Goat Man hiding in some basement. She'd seen it shot multiple times, and even though the bullets didn't bring it down, they had to have done some kind of damage, no matter how minor. If it – Jason – needed to rest and recharge, it would go back to the woods where it had been brought to life.

"How many exorcisms have you done?" Chad asked as they skirted around a pile of crushed cars that had been tossed into the middle of an intersection.

Father Farmer kept his eyes ahead. "None."

"None?" Samantha said.

"It's not a common thing in the Catholic church. If you were looking for someone with experience, you should have tried the Pentecostal church on the other side of town. I hear they make a big show of it every Sunday."

Tina jumped the curb to avoid a truck lying on its side. "I'm not assigned to feeding any Pentecostal priests."

His fingers thrummed on the dashboard. "Well, lucky me."

"Do you know how to do one?" Chad said.

"To be an official exorcist requires special training. Not much call for it and not many priests have the proper qualifications."

Samantha felt her spirits, already down in the murky depths, sink even lower. "I guess we should have asked you that before we brought you along."

The old priest turned around to face her. "Even if I was a trained exorcist, it's not like there would have been any secret passages about how to battle a Goat Man. I've been around long enough to know that you can pretty much wing anything as long as you have some modicum of intelligence and common sense."

Chad raised his hands. "Great. We'll just wing it."

Samantha cast her gaze onto her lap where her hands were clasped tightly together. When she'd last checked her phone, she saw that the Whataburger gathering had been pushed up to noon. They had to find Jason before the mob. Even if they did, would they be able to do anything to help him? Or was Samantha about to get her best friend, a priest and a podcaster murdered? It sounded like the start to some terrible joke.

"Are you sure about this?" Tina asked Samantha.

At first, Samantha had no idea what she was talking about. Then she saw what street they were on and where it would take them. "I'm not sure about anything anymore, but I think this is our best bet."

Chad stared nervously out the window. He had mumbled something earlier about seeing Michael's body again. It must have been hard for him, and she gave him credit for sticking with them this far.

Of course, he had said he was going to grab his camera and film the exorcism. Samantha just hoped he'd put the thing down if they were in trouble and needed his help. She had no desire to be in a found footage horror movie.

They drove by a gathering of people working at a sewer cap with a crowbar.

"Where did they find all those guns?" Chad mused.

"It's Texas," Tina replied, and that's all that needed to be said.

Part of Samantha wished they had a gun, too, but then she thought of Jason and how she wouldn't spoil any chance to save him, even if the Goat Man scared the living crap out of her.

Several minutes later, they pulled into the parking lot beside the entrance to the path to the Goat Man's Bridge. The lot was empty...for now. Sooner or later, the posse would arrive, hungry for blood. Tina slowly drove up and over the curb and onto the path itself. When they were a dozen or so feet from the bridge, she stopped and opened her door. "The car will block the angry villagers from getting through here easily."

Father Farmer took one look at Michael's broken body and said a quick, silent prayer.

"Was he your friend?" he asked Chad.

Chad inhaled deeply and bit his top lip. "Yeah."

The priest put a hand on his shoulder. "I'm sorry for your loss."

Tina urged them forward. "Let's make sure you don't have to feel sorry for a lot more losses." She led the way, with Samantha by her side. They had to keep glancing back to make sure Father Farmer could keep up. That also meant they had to take it slower than they would have liked.

"Can't have him dropping dead," Tina whispered to Samantha.

"That would be just our luck."

Chad told them where to turn, assuming the Goat Man was back where the Satanic ritual had taken place. It was a gamble coming out here. First, they were going to a hellish hot zone. Second, if they were wrong and the Goat Man was somewhere else, the gun-toting citizens would do their best to make quick work of the beast. Samantha was sure she spotted someone back by the sewer opening wearing a vest full of hand grenades clipped to the front. And the long tube-like gun someone else had looked like some kind of rocket launcher.

As they worked their way through the trees, she couldn't help notice the complete absence of sound. There wasn't a single bird in the sky or critter on the ground. As eerie as it was, it gave her hope that they were on the right track.

CHAPTER TWENTY

The Goat Man stirred, opening his crusted eyes. Someone was coming. The great beast stretched its limbs, felt the blood rushing through its veins, restoring its strength. This terrestrial body, as strong as it was, had limitations, and that made the Goat Man seethe. If only it could wantonly spread death and chaos without cease, that would be this side of inglorious hell.

All of the vegetation around it had perished and blackened. When it leaned against the tree to stand, the doomed thing groaned and toppled over, shattering into onyx chips.

The sun shined above, hurting the Goat Man's eyes. It wished for darkness, but it could no longer slumber.

Death needed to be dealt, whether they called its name or not.

Lou was grateful she avoided sewer detail. All those people tramping around down there were in for all kinds of infections. Just disgusting.

Her team leader's phone beeped constantly as messages and calls came in. He had a woman with stringy hair sticking out of the band of her trucker cap that Lou assumed was his wife marking things off on a map after every check in.

Currently, they were combing the alleys in a section of town that was crammed with low rise apartment buildings.

All Lou had found so far was a lot of garbage, little baggies that must have once contained drugs, a few deflated condoms and a scurrying mouse that had her reaching for her gun. Luckily, she stopped herself from pulling the trigger. If she was jumpy enough to shoot at a mouse, they'd probably send her home, worried that she might shoot one of the posse.

They'd be smart to be concerned.

Her biggest concern was that they would lose daylight. Facing that thing under cover of night invoked pants-pissing terror.

She couldn't shake the feeling that they were way off track. As much as the Goat Man scared her, she felt safe surrounded by these people and their weapons. When the Goat Man was caught, she didn't want to miss out.

Which is why she needed to speak to the team leader. She thought he'd said his name was Jon. He was a pretty big and intimidating guy with a booming voice and a chin that could crush beer cans. Jon's body seemed to expand with each passing moment, filled with the importance of being in charge of the group. He reminded Lou of every principal she'd ever had.

Cautiously, she approached Jon and his map-toting wife. "Excuse me?"

They turned on her, guns at the ready. "Jesus, kid, you could have gotten yourself killed sneaking up on us like that."

Lou didn't think she had snuck up on them in the slightest. In fact, she had made it a point to drag her feet and kick a rock just to make some noise and alert them she was coming.

They're just as wired as I am.

"I…I'm sorry. It's just, I think we're looking in the wrong place."

Jon smiled at her the way adults smiled at dumb kids who say even dumber things. "No stone unturned. You never know where that thing might pop up."

"I might know where it is."

His wife looked skeptical, making it a point to focus back on the map.

"Oh?" Jon's eyebrow went up. "And how would that be?"

Lou swallowed and wished she had a bottle of water. "Well, I uh, I was in the woods out by the Goat Man's Bridge when it chased me and my boyfriend." Her eyes burned when she said, "It killed him."

Jon leaned against the building. "Is that so?"

"Yes. It chased me several times last night. I wasn't alone, there were some other people I met up with. One of them is this podcaster whose partner was killed right on the bridge."

A small smile crept onto his face. "You say it chased you *several* times? And you, above everyone else in this town, lived to tell about it? How is that?"

Great. He didn't believe her. Lou had dealt with enough asshole adults to know there was no convincing him. She kind of wished she'd stayed with Samantha and Tina. But then again, they had different plans for this day.

Instead of wasting oxygen, she sighed and said, "Never mind. I'll just go find it on my own."

"I wouldn't advise you to go out on your own, missy. You could get hurt. And not just by that demon. There are a lot of trigger happy people out and about."

Trigger happy people that, like Jon, wouldn't believe her.

"I'll be fine," she snapped. "And if you get tired of poking around alleys, you can find me, and the demon, in the woods. Unless you're too scared."

She saw the flash of shock on his face and turned around and walked away before he could say something to insult her.

These people were plain stupid. There was a Goat Man running around killing everyone, so why weren't they all at the very bridge named after it?

Maybe because deep down, they didn't really want to find it. They saw what the Goat Man did to the town. This could all be a lot of chest beating and bluster. Come nightfall, they'd get in their trucks and head for the hills.

"Screw them."

Lou walked away from them and stuck her thumb out for a ride. She made sure to unbutton her shirt a little and push out her chest. Sure enough, a Ram truck driven by a good ole' boy pulled over to the curb. He had a rifle lying on the dashboard. "It's awfully dangerous out here for a cutie like you," he said. He had curly hair and a drooping mustache. She bet he had a beer gut straining against his oversized belt buckle.

"I need a ride to the Goat Man's Bridge. You think you can take me?"

He tapped the side of his door. "Today's your lucky day, if there's any luck to be had. I was heading over there to meet up with some other folks. Hop in."

She climbed into the passenger seat and was surprised to see his flat belly. No belt buckle visible, either.

"Name's Shane," he said. "You want me to take you home instead?"

She flashed her gun. "I'm in this like the rest of you. And I know where to find it."

Shane tipped his baseball cap. "If you're right, I'm damn glad to meet you."

CHAPTER TWENTY-ONE

Chad preferred to view their trek through the woods to the place where the Satanists had brought the Goat Man to life through the viewfinder of his camera. Scratch that. Michael's camera. It helped remove him slightly from the reality of what was happening, affording him a counterfeit feeling of slim security.

He did his best not to jangle it too much and give future viewers a case of the Blair Witch nausea. Because he was focused on Samantha, Tina and the priest, he wasn't watching where he was stepping and nearly toppled ass over teakettle when he tripped on tree roots and rocks or dipped into holes in the ground.

"You might want to be more careful," Tina said when he extracted his foot from one of those holes. "Snakes make those holes. Unless you like snakes."

Point in fact, Chad despised snakes. Were there rattlesnakes in this part of Texas? Of course, there had to be. This place had a Goat Man, so why not venomous snakes?

"Are we almost there?" Samantha asked. She held onto Father Farmer's hand to keep him from falling.

The lead feeling in Chad's gut was all he needed to know they were close. That and the fact that everything here was dead. It hadn't been when he'd come here before. That was all the proof he needed that the Goat Man was near.

"Yeah. Should be just up ahead."

And I should be running like hell in the other direction, Chad thought.

No, he was going to do this, not for the potential fame and fortune – though that would be nice – but for Michael. Chad wished he could be here to see this. Michael would have been fearless.

They walked for a couple more minutes, popping out of the dead tree line when Samantha stopped and raised her hand for everyone else to do the same. "Oh."

Chad saw the Goat Man striding across the field, headed straight for them with the confident gait of an 80's slasher. He thought the moment called for more than a meek, "Oh."

"Fuck me," he whispered, keeping his focus on what the camera was showing him. He zoomed in on the Goat Man. Was it bigger than before? Or was that just because he was looking at it in full daylight? No, it looked taller, broader. Even its horns seemed thicker.

The heat of the sun sent wisps of steam off its shoulders. It looked none too happy to have visitors.

"Now what do we do?" Chad said.

Father Farmer saw the creature and said, "Shit in my hat and call it the blue plate special."

Chad had the presence of mind to capture the reactions of Tina, Samantha and the priest. They were all pretty similar – mouths open, eyes wide, with a heavy dose of terror.

"Should you be saying some kind of prayer or something?" Tina said.

"I don't honestly think a Hail Mary is going to do us much good. You failed to mention it was so…so big!"

"I'm not sure size is the issue here," Tina said.

Samantha took a step forward. "He won't hurt me."

Tina reached for her hand. "He *didn't* hurt you last night. It looks different today. I think it's safe to say this was a very bad idea. We should go. And when I say go, I mean run."

Slipping out of Tina's grasp, Samantha took another step. This seemed to perplex the Goat Man, because the creature slowed its pace.

"Jason's in there."

Now, Chad was in lockstep with Tina. The huge fly in the ointment was the elderly priest. He was in no condition to run, and Chad was in no shape to carry him. As much as he hated to admit it, this would have to be their last stand. All of his faith was in Samantha now, and the remnants of the connection with her boyfriend.

Chad thought this was the time to turn the camera around and say something, maybe tell his parents he loved them, or speak about the sacrifice he was making for the people who would watch this video later. Maybe he should scream that the Goat Man was real and to run and hide.

There was no way he could steal the shot away from Samantha and she slowly walked toward the Goat Man. Tina pleaded for her to stop. Father Farmer set his briefcase on the ground and knelt before it. He kissed a green stole and placed it around his neck so it rested down the sides of his chest. His hand shook as it held a battered Bible, the other palming a small glass vial.

"In the name of the Father, and of the Son, and the Holy Spirit. Amen."

The priest prayed while Samantha went to meet the Goat Man. Instead of charging her, it walked slowly, warily.

"This is so not good," Tina said, worrying at the ends of her hair.

"We're nuts to ever think it would be," Chad said.

Father Farmer read passages from his Bible.

Samantha stopped. "Jason. Jason, can you hear me?"

The Goat Man stopped as well. It cocked its horned head.

"Jason, I need you to come to me." A warm wind passed through the field. It felt as if it had come straight from the Goat Man's steaming flesh. "Come, Jason. We'll help you. We can save you."

Chad had a hard time keeping the camera from shaking. He'd always thought knees knocking sounded ridiculous and impossible. Not so, now. His kneecaps sounded like maracas.

Samantha and the Goat Man were only separated by ten yards at the most. It looked like they were standing in the middle of a landing zone decimated by extreme heat.

"That's right, Jason. It's me, Samantha. If you can, if you can just take control, we can work on getting you free."

She's either the bravest or craziest person who ever walked the Earth.

Chad slid the focus to the Goat Man's face, zeroing in on its red eyes. If Jason was in there, he didn't see it. It was like staring into a fiery cauldron.

When Samantha raised her hand, the Goat Man's hands curled into fists.

"Sam, look out," Chad shouted.

She turned around.

Tina ran to her friend. The Goat Man skirted around Samantha and slammed Tina with the back of its hand. Her body went airborne. Chad tried to follow her flight, but she disappeared into some nearby bushes.

"Tina!" Father Farmer hobbled after her.

She's dead, Chad thought. *No way she survived a Goat Man bitch slap like that*. In a way, it might have shown her mercy.

Samantha looked over to where Tina had vanished in the brush, her eyes brimming with tears. "Jason!" she screamed. "What have you done?"

The Goat Man sneered at Samantha. Whatever had existed between them last night was gone. He could see it in the beast's soulless eyes. Any second now, it would rip her head clean off. Chad had to do something.

"Hey, over here!" he called out, waving one arm while still filming.

The Goat Man's head snapped in his direction. Chad's bowels liquified. The creature roared and started to charge. Chad dropped the camera and immediately tripped over his own feet.

Just before the Goat Man could tear him to pieces, Father Farmer erupted from the brush, flicking his hand in the monster's direction and chanting, "Get back! Get back, vile beast!"

Something hissed on the Goat Man's flesh and hair, and it howled in pain, staggering backward until it bowled into Samantha.

Lou heard the inhuman howl and turned to Shane. "You hear that?"

He tightened his grip on his rifle. "People in Mexico heard that."

They'd joined a couple of dozen people sent to check out the Goat Man's Bridge by a completely separate crew of vigilantes. They had all arrived in enormous pickup trucks and had so many huge guns, Lou thought she had stepped onto the set of *Predator*.

"It's out there, just like I said."

Shane put an iron hand on her shoulder. "I'll lead the way. You just stick close to me and tell me which way to go."

The sun's glare was weakening in the sky.

She urged Shane forward. "Go. We don't have time to waste."

They crossed the empty lot and came to the path to the infamous Goat Man's Bridge, a landmark destined to become the stuff of real nightmares for generations. Lou recalled all the times she had come out here for a cheap thrill, never truly believing the stupid legend. Even after all she'd been through, she still didn't. If that Goat Man, the one that had gone all psycho Hulk on everyone, had been out there since the 1800s, it would have made its presence known long before now.

This Goat Man was an imposter, but a damn destructive one at that. It had made her an orphan. Now she wanted to make it a corpse.

They came to a car blocking the path to the bridge. It sounded liked someone was pounding on the trunk to get out. Lou recognized the car as the one Tina had stolen. Which could only mean that disgusting Lupita was inside.

Everyone else was too fixated on the Goat Man's wails to pay it any mind. They filed around the car and took to the bridge. Shane paused and looked to Lou. "Should I knock and call out for it?"

"Don't be a dumbass."

She could tell that wasn't the response he was hoping for.

Lou couldn't care less. She had two worries.

One, that Samantha might find a way to stop the Goat Man and save her boyfriend.

Two, that she had failed and now her, Tina and Chad were chop meat.

The well-armed crew crossed the bridge, some of them seeing Michael's body and talking loudly about what they were going to do to the monster when they found it.

Not before I get my shot in, Lou thought.

CHAPTER TWENTY-TWO

Samantha tried to swallow her heart down from the middle of her throat. She looked all around for Tina and couldn't find her.

Had she been wrong? Was Jason too far gone to save?

"Tina!"

She could only watch helplessly as the Goat Man charged for Chad. There was no point wasting the distraction. She had to find Tina.

After only a couple of steps toward where she thought Tina lay, Samantha was knocked off her feet as the Goat Man barreled into her. She tumbled end over end, the wind knocked out of her, the sounds of the Goat Man's cries hurting her ears.

Coming to a rest on her side, her hand went to her ribs, wondering if they were cracked or broken. Her vision danced for a few moments as she regained her equilibrium.

When she could focus again, her eyes laid upon the supine form of the Goat Man. It twisted its head to look directly at her. What burned within those eyes made her pee run freely.

No! Jason's gone! We have to get out of here!

It took a great deal of effort to get up. At one point, the stabbing pain in her lungs nearly dropped her like a linebacker.

To her surprise, the Goat Man remained on the ground.

"Tina!" she wheezed.

Chad came running to her with his camera up and filming the whole thing. "Did you fucking see that?"

"What? What?" She hadn't even seen the Goat Man crash into her.

Father Farmer brought up the rear, wielding a half-empty bottle of what she supposed was holy water. "Take this, dear," he said, stuffing his Bible in her hands and huffing and puffing his way to the fallen creature. "And you, by the power of God, maker of the heavens, remain bound to the Earth!" He splashed the Goat Man's chest with holy water. Its head reared from the ground and it let out a bellow that rivaled the power of a foghorn.

Samantha backed away with her right hand over one ear and the Bible over the other. The Goat Man thrashed on the ground as Father Farmer doused it with more holy water.

"The Bible," the priest said.

Samantha was rooted to the spot, staring at the creature and the strange mist coming off its body.

"Samantha dear, come here and open the Bible for me. Now!"

She shook as if being woken from a deep sleep and shambled next to the priest. Chad had to step out of the way, taking a position now over her shoulder.

"I need you to keep it open for me," Father Farmer said, rifling through the pages. "Can you do that?"

She nodded.

The priest put his finger on the page and began reading, his voice rising as he went along. "*And when Jesus came into the country of the Gergesenes, he met two men possessed by devils, coming out of the tombs, exceedingly fierce, so that no man may pass that way.*"

The Goat Man bleated and growled. It was enough to bring them to their knees. Samantha thought of poor Jason, possessed by a devil right now, and how his fierce cries would prevent any rational person from coming within fifty miles of this location.

"And behold, they cried out saying, What have we to do with Jesus, Son of God? Have you only come here to torment us?"

"I wonder when he gets to the whole power of Christ compelling it to do stuff," Chad whispered behind her. Samantha wanted to smack him.

She dared to look at the Goat Man again, as if she were willing her resolve not to break. As the priest read from the Bible, she saw a completely new expression on its face, in its eyes that had dimmed considerably.

Pain. Confusion.

The crimson in its eyes roiled and rolled away, like passing clouds, and behind that blood red sheathing were pale, blue orbs.

Like Jason's eyes!

"It...hurts," the Goat Man said, only with Jason's voice.

It reached out for her, but she wasn't bold enough to take its hand. All she could do was say, "Keep going, Father." Above all, she could pray, and hope it was working.

When Tina came to, the sun was dancing in the sky. She had to blink repeatedly to get it to stay in one place.

Next, the flare of pain in her arm called out to her. She looked down and saw her forearm was tilted in a way that should not have been possible.

It took her a bit of struggling to disentangle herself from the shrub that she had landed within. Sharp branches did a fine job cutting up her face and neck, the awkwardness of it all making her move her broken arm in ways it didn't want to move, sending fresh flashes of agony.

Looking to her left, she saw a pile of dead bodies stacked on one another like slices of meat in a whopper of a sandwich. They all wore police uniforms. Their necks had been torn open and bits of the inner parts cooled on their outer parts. Tina thought she was going to be sick.

Once she was free from the denuded shrub, she spied upon the Goat Man on its back, its flesh and fur billowing with smoke whenever Father Farmer hit it with holy water.

Holy shit! It was working!

Samantha looked like she was about to pass out, standing there holding the Bible open like an altar server. Chad was filming the exorcism where he should have been lending them a hand somehow.

When it spoke in Jason's voice again, Tina lost her breath. For as long as she lived, she would never be able to fully reconcile that voice coming from that creature. Then it bayed in agony and anger and Tina thought it was going to leap up and swipe at them. Father Farmer sprinkled more holy water and that seemed to settle it down.

At least something was working against the demonic beast.

But Tina also noticed that there was very little left in the bottle. How long would it be able to hold out? She recalled watching a documentary on exorcisms and how they could take hours, if not days, weeks or months. And that was just a run of the mill possession of a person. If the Goat Man could be exorcised, how long would it take? Years?

They didn't have that kind of time.

What was needed here was something on a grand scale to match the enormity of the situation.

Tina knew she should go over there and let Sam know she was alive.

But there was something else more important she should do, and very little time to do it. She ran, holding her broken arm, hoping she could pull it off before it was too late.

CHAPTER TWENTY-THREE

"That's gotta be it!" Shane exclaimed. His face had paled a bit, as had everyone else's, but they continued on.

"Trust me, it is," Lou said. She'd heard similar sounds the night before, though this time around, the Goat Man sounded more wounded than murderous. They needed to double time it. She overtook Shane at the lead and started jogging. "Hurry."

The revenge party formed a single line trying to keep up with her. Some were burdened with heavy weaponry and fell to the back of the pack.

Whatever Samantha was doing must be working. Lou wondered just how Sam's boyfriend was supposed to magically separate from the Goat Man's body. It didn't seem possible. Then again, a towering Goat Man wreaking havoc on their town didn't seem possible twenty-four hours ago.

Even if Sam pulled off the impossible, maybe there would be something left of the demonic side of the creature for her to take her anger out on. She sure hoped so.

They'd made it to the copse of trees, following the bellows of the Goat Man as a living GPS, when Tina came running toward them. Lou saw the angle of her arm and winced, feeling sympathy pains. Tina saw Lou, and then the people behind her, and stopped.

"You need to go back," Tina said breathlessly. Her face was covered in fat beads of sweat.

"From the looks of you, we need to keep on going," Shane said.

"No!" She fixed her eyes on Lou. "Something's happening back there. It's working. But I need to give it a little boost. Promise me you won't go barging over there like a bunch of crazed cowboys."

"What's working?" Lou asked.

"The exorcism. We have a priest with us. Look, you just have to trust me on this. Stay here in case it doesn't work, because if they fail, that thing is coming back to the scene of its crimes. You can stop it here." Tina's eyes flicked from weapon to weapon. "Looks like you have enough to take on Afghanistan." She grabbed Lou's arm. "Promise me you'll stay right here. Set a trap for it if you want."

"I promise," Lou said. "Where are you going?"

"Not far. I'll be right back."

With that, Tina hustled back the way they'd come, keeping her busted arm close to her body.

They all watched her go, giving her a wide berth.

"So," Shane said. "Do we wait here?"

"No. We're almost there. Let's get this over with."

Father Farmer flipped to the Gospel of Luke and read more passages, all while flicking more holy water on the Goat Man. He asked Chad to get his briefcase. Chad never put his camera down.

"Hand me that crucifix."

Chad took the simple wooden crucifix with a golden Jesus out of a pocket in the briefcase and gave it to the priest.

The Bible felt as if it weighed a metric ton in Samantha's trembling arms. The Goat Man was flashing between two states – the demonic entity that had melded the chimera, and the man she loved, in obvious pain and desperate for help.

"Is it working?" Samantha asked.

"We're still here, so that's a good sign," Father Farmer said. "I need you to talk to it. I mean, talk to your boyfriend. Keep him focused so he can fight from within."

Pain lanced in her side. She nearly dropped the Bible. "J-Jason. Honey, just keep fighting. We're going to get you out. But I need you to fight."

Father Farmer took a daring step closer and pressed the crucifix to the Goat Man's forehead, right between its horns. The stench of burning fur filled the air. This time, the Goat Man did lash out, catching the priest on the thigh. He fell sideways. The crucifix was jarred from his hand and slid under a pile of ash that until recently had been lush, green grass.

"Chad, put that camera down and help him!" Samantha barked.

"Yeah, yeah. Sorry." She noticed he set the camera carefully on the ground, making sure to keep the Goat Man in the frame. Father Farmer was slow getting up.

Samantha's eyes bulged when the Goat Man started to sit up, its eyes reddening.

"Um, Father?"

The priest fumbled for the holy water and spritzed the Goat Man, sending it on its back again.

"Maybe don't do the whole cross on the head thing again," Chad said as he retrieved his camera.

"That is most advisable," Father Farmer replied, his voice sounding shaky.

He leaned into Samantha as he looked for a new passage in the Bible.

The three of them jumped when they heard the crack of gunfire.

Samantha spun around, painfully, and saw the group of people emerge from the trees. They looked like an army of mercenaries.

And they were led by Lou!

"Lou? What are you doing?"

The teen walked confidently across the barren field. "I'm doing what needs to be done. We all are." She gestured toward her entourage. "I mean, look at this place. You think an old priest is going to stop it?"

Samantha pointed at the prone Goat Man. "Look for yourself. If we weren't close, you think we wouldn't all be dead by now?"

"I think you need to step away from that thing and let us handle it."

Samantha couldn't believe it. Where was the frightened kid from just a night ago? Sure, there was safety in numbers – and weapons in this case – but Lou seemed like a different person.

"Lou, see for yourself," Chad said. "It can be hurt. Show them, Father."

The priest's hand trembled violently as he put his thumb over the top of the vial of holy water. Like most people, he obviously didn't like having guns pointed at him.

He turned to dash more holy water on the Goat Man when a shot buzzed past his left ear. The bullet hit the Goat Man, but didn't penetrate its flesh. The flattened slug bounced along the blackened ground.

"No!" Samantha shouted a moment before the priest dragged her onto the ground.

The wasteland of a field was filled with the booming of gunfire. She heard Chad grunt, saw his camera explode into bits of glass, plastic and metal, and watched him fall, half of his face missing.

The sudden assault eradicated everything Father Farmer had done. It only angered the Goat Man, who was now on its two cloven hooves. It grabbed ahold of the nearest dead tree, yanked it out by its roots, and threw it with incredible velocity at the vigilantes. Most either dropped or scattered, but two men took the charred trunk straight to their faces. The heavy weight obliterated their heads on impact. One headless body fell, while the other stumbled around for a few nauseating steps before tripping on a rock. When it hit the ground, blood and gore pumped freely from the exposed neck hole.

The Goat Man's body was scarred by the holy water, but its eyes gleamed red and smoke blasted from its nostrils. It absorbed shot after shot, some of them pinging off its horns.

Samantha and the priest crawled on their bellies to get out of the line of fire. She thought of screaming at Lou to stop but knew there was no getting through to her or the other vigilantes. Even watching two of their own go down violently hadn't gotten them to turn tail and run. In fact, they had stepped up their assault.

Lowering its head so its horns took the brunt of their fire, the Goat Man charged them.

It caught a woman square in her chest. Her entire body exploded, as if she had been made of paper – paper filled with a copious amount of red Jell-O. The others scrambled so they could fire directly into the Goat Man's torso. Samantha saw a geyser of blood erupt from one of the wounds as some hand cannon went off like a sonic boom.

They were going to kill it! Not it. Jason!

The worst part was, there was nothing she could do. She turned to Father Farmer. "Can you help me pray?"

He took her hand in his and started reciting the Lord's Prayer.

CHAPTER TWENTY-FOUR

Lou fired a shot at the Goat Man's hide, but it seemed to do very little. Only Shane, with a gun that looked like some fake thing from a movie, had had any effect on the monster.

"Take that, motherfucker!" Shane shouted gleefully.

He took aim, pointing at the bleeding wound. The Goat Man caught his arm with a backwards kick. One moment, Shane's arm was there holding the huge gun, the next, it was gone. He spiraled through the dead trees, spurting blood and mumbling incoherently. Lou ran to see if there was any way to save him. The arm was gone clear to his shoulder. Short of cauterizing the gushing wound, there was no way to stop the bleeding.

Shane slumped against a tree. His eyes rolled to her. "Take…take my gun." He didn't realize his gun and arm were somewhere in the distance. "Kill it…for me."

His breath gurgled and his chest went still.

Lou wished she had his gun. It was obvious her father's pistol was no better than a pea shooter.

The screaming at her back stopped her from searching for it. They were hitting the Goat Man with everything they had, and it only seemed to be making it angrier. The air was pungent with gunpowder and cordite. Her ears were ringing, and for moments, all she could hear was the thudding of her own heart.

How was it still standing?

She watched it tear into a man, cracking his ribcage open with a blow from its fist and then tearing his innards out like a dog digging for a lost bone.

The wound Shane had given it was clear as day. Open and red and seeping blood.

There was only one thing to do.

Lou ran toward the Goat Man, screeching like a lunatic. She jumped onto its back and grabbed onto its coarse fur just as it reared up and tried to shake her off.

Jamming her gun deep enough into the wound so her wrist was no longer visible, she pulled the trigger once, twice, until the third time produced a dull click.

The Goat Man howled, clutching its chest.

"I hope those bullets found your black fucking heart!" Lou shouted close to its ear.

It snapped its head back. Lou's head crunched like a cracker as a horn split her skull in two. She slid, lifeless, off its body, dead before she could witness reinforcements coming, having followed the cacophony of death and destruction.

Samantha turned her head just in time to see more men, women, and even some children come pouring through the trees. The first group was mostly dead or dying, but how much longer could the Goat Man stand?

She stifled a gasp when she saw Lou's corpse in a tangled heap. Her head was in two pieces. The poor girl.

Then she looked over at Chad and wondered if there was a place where he and Michael would reunite. After all the evil she had seen, there had to be its polar opposite, somewhere. She had watched the good in Father Farmer lay the Goat Man on its back. That had to count for something.

Tina was somewhere in the field, more than likely dead, because if she had been alive, she would have come to Samantha by now. Or maybe she was too hurt to move.

Samantha wanted the shooting to stop so she could get up and find her best friend.

They were all doomed. Of that, she was certain.

When she died, would she ever see Jason again? Never a believer in heaven or hell, everything she had felt she had known had been ripped out from under her. Did Jason have one foot in the Goat Man, and the other in hell? He'd been such a good, caring man. Would a just God let him suffer for eternity?

There were too many existential questions to consider when what she really needed to do was find a way out of this place.

The air around the Goat Man grew hazy, and it lifted its arms around the piles of dead people. Slowly, jerkily, they got to their feet. Even Lou, whose sides of her head separated even further, exposing her wet brain speckled with burned bits of grass and soil.

"What in the name of God?" Samantha gasped.

"God has nothing to do with this," Father Farmer said.

At the sight of the beast raising the dead, the latest group of vigilantes ceased fire, transfixed by the unholy display.

"Come," Father Farmer said, pulling on Samantha's arm. "We'll find a place to hide."

She didn't think there was anywhere on Earth they could hide. Jason would find her.

She felt a rumbling beneath her feet.

Wood cracked and trees collapsed in the near distance.

Someone shouted, "Get out of the way! Run!"

A huge truck exploded out of the charred trees, hitting the Goat Man and some of the twitching dead with the front grill. They scattered like bowling pins, one of the dead men pinwheeling just past Samantha and Father Farmer, coating them with his blood.

The truck kept coming, the massive back wheels rolling over the fallen Goat Man. Samantha thought for sure it was going to hit them.

It came to a skidding stop, engine rumbling.

The door cracked open.

Tina jumped out of the cab, wincing with pain and cradling her arm.

"Tina!" Samantha threw her arms around her.

"Ow, shit that hurts." Tina pulled away. "We can hug later, when I'm in a hospital doped up on meds." She turned to the priest. "You think you can make all of this holy?"

Samantha looked at the side of the truck. It said, in bright blue letters, Rink Pools. It was one of those tanker trucks that delivered pool water. There had to be thousands of gallons in the tank.

Father Farmer looked the truck up and down with wide eyes. "I don't make it holy. The Lord does."

"Well, you think you can get him to give us a freakin' hand?" Tina said.

Samantha saw the Goat Man struggling to get to its feet. She nudged the priest toward the truck.

"I can certainly try," he said. With one hand flat on the side of the tank, he closed his eyes, made the sign of the cross, and proceeded to bless the water within. When he was done, he said Amen, and started all over again.

"He sees us," Samantha said. She was sure there was no way of getting through to Jason now. The battered and bruised monster stared at them with death in its cold, red eyes.

"Hurry up, Father," Tina said.

"An extra prayer can't hurt," he said before continuing.

Tina opened the catch on the side of the truck and asked Samantha to help her with the hose. They unrolled it and pulled the nozzle end to the back of the truck.

"You're going to have to hold onto it," Tina said. "I can't do much with one arm. You just need to grip it tight. Okay?"

Samantha nodded fervently, her eyes fixed on the Goat Man.

"Amen!" Father Farmer shouted.

Tina worked the handle to release the water.

Samantha felt pressure building in the hose.

The Goat Man bleated, baring its bloody teeth.

As soon as the water jettisoned out of the hose, Samantha shouted, "Give me back my Jason!"

The geyser hit the Goat Man in the chest, dousing it in seconds. It dropped to its knees as the steady stream of water rapidly turned to steam. Within the flowing water, the beast writhed and undulated, but couldn't escape. Father Farmer shouted prayers over the rushing of the water while Samantha desperately tried to keep the stream aimed on the beast. She felt bone scrape on bone in her ribcage and grew faint, but held firm.

Gallons and gallons of holy water drenched the Goat Man.

The vigilantes who had come to deliver mob justice backed away, sensing something more powerful than anything their weapons could provide was in play.

Tina came to Samantha's side and took hold of the hose with her good arm. "Just keep it coming until there's nothing left."

The ground shook beneath their feet.

Trees, already dead, toppled. The vigilantes scattered.

The Goat Man unleashed a torrent of wet, gurgling wails.

Less and less steam filled the air.

A zig-zag crack split the ground between the truck and the Goat Man. Samantha wondered how much longer before it opened wide enough to swallow the truck...and them!

Then, out of the bath of holy water, they heard a voice.

"Samantha."

It was weak and sad and desperate.

"Jason?"

"Yes. Help me."

"It could be a trap," Tina warned her.

"Father, can you hold this?"

The priest ambled over and took the hose. "Tina could be right."

Samantha said, "I don't care anymore," and ran the distance between them, making sure to avoid the fissure. Holy water poured into it, and she thought she saw it sealing back up.

The spray from the hose flattened her hair and penetrated her clothes.

Only a few feet away, she turned to Tina and Father Farmer and shouted, "Stop. I need to see!"

The form beneath the water was much smaller than it had been before.

"Samantha, please."

Her heart leapt. Any second now, the water would turn off and her Jason would be back with her. For the first time in her life, she believed in miracles.

The water cut off.

"Thank you, baby. Thank you."

The Goat Man collapsed, his face splashing into a puddle of water.

Samantha screamed, and then she passed out.

The slap of something ice cold brought Jason to the fore of the Goat Man. He savored the cooling water as it pummeled his hideous form to the ground.

He knew Samantha was close by, and he needed her now more than ever. He called to her, desperate to hear her voice, to feel her touch, to know not only that she was alright, but there to give him comfort.

Horrid images flashed across his mind, displays of the atrocities the Goat Man had committed.

What *he* had committed.

"Thank you, baby. Thank you."

The heavy cascade of water ceased and Jason, on his hands and knees now, looked up and saw Samantha standing before him. He wanted to leap up and take her in his arms, grateful that the nightmare was over.

Unmitigated terror in her eyes, Samantha shrieked and collapsed.

Jason struggled to get up to come to her aid. For the first time in what felt like an eternity, he wasn't plagued by the urge to kill.

As he pushed himself up, he saw hands that were not his own.

It was then he saw his reflection in the pooling water.

The face of a goat stared back at him.

"Don't you fucking touch her!"

Shutting his eyes against the nightmare image, he turned away and opened them to see Tina and a priest holding a giant hose connected to a tanker truck. They were both visibly hurt and in pain and Jason knew he had been the cause of it.

As he took in the blackened field around him, he saw corpses in various states of ruin everywhere.

The Goat Man, or the vile thing that had been within Jason and this miserable body, was gone. Of that, he was sure.

But so was Jason's body. What had been done apparently could not be undone.

He would forever be a monster.

Locking eyes with Tina, he said, "Take…take care of her. Please."

His legs unsteady, Jason rose and walked away, not wanting Samantha to see him when she regained consciousness. Heartbroken, soul forever tainted, Jason kept walking until the forest swallowed him whole.

Chapter Twenty-Five

"What do we do with it?" Tina used a wire hanger to scratch under her cast.

"I don't know. And honestly, I don't care." Samantha sat on the steps outside her apartment building with her arms crossed over her knees.

"Well, that stink is never getting out of that car."

"It's not even your car."

"True. But still. It was a person at one time."

"A bad person that fucked up more lives than you or I can count."

The streets were quiet in the weeks following the Goat Man's birth and rampage. FEMA had been dispatched to the town, along with the National Guard to help put things back together. But Samantha knew no matter what they did, this place was broken forever.

"You want to go see him?" Tina asked.

"I do. But, is it safe?"

"People have more important things to do. And I don't think anyone's heading out that way anytime soon. Come on."

Tina had been right. The car reeked. They kept all the windows open as they drove. At one point Tina turned the radio on, but Samantha quickly shut it off.

They came to the all too familiar parking lot behind the strip mall. The brakes squealed and Tina was the first one out, taking deep breaths of clean air. "You want me to go with you?"

Samantha shut the door behind her. "No. I'll be fine."

"You sure?"

"I don't think I'll ever be sure about anything."

She walked across the lot to the path, listening to birdsong and wishing she could just fly away.

Tina opened the trunk and ran back to avoid the wall of fetid air. After keeping upwind for several minutes, she walked over and looked inside.

Lupita looked just as bad as she had weeks ago. Apparently, she didn't need to eat or drink. How *did* one care for a burned blob?

"Pleeaassssse killlll mmmmmeeeee."

"You realize if I kill you, you'll probably go straight to hell."

"Ohhhhh, yesssss."

"Fucking weird. Sorry I kind of forgot about you. We had a lot going on."

Lupita's wandering eye rolled and rolled. Tina didn't know what that could possibly mean. And, truth be told, she didn't care.

"Alrighty. Have it your way."

She opened the back door and took out the broom handle. She'd duct taped a very sharp chef's knife to the end.

Just as she was about to stab it into Lupita, she stopped. "You know, I really should just chuck you in the sewer and let you suffer."

Lupita didn't respond. Just that eye, staring at her.

"Then again, you're kinda gross and I don't want to make the rats sick."

The knife slid into Lupita's eye with ease. Tina moved the knife around, not sure if there were any organs she needed to sever to put the blob out of her misery. Or send her to an eternity of misery. Whatever.

When Lupita stopped quivering, Tina lifted the handle out with Lupita stuck to the end. She carried it to a spot off the path and went back to the car to fetch her shovel.

Samantha stopped in the middle of the bridge and watched the water rush beneath it. The wood was still stained with Michael's blood. The Internet was in mourning over the hosts of the Monstrous Places podcast and all of the people lost.

Taking a deep breath, Samantha made a fist.

She knocked on the red rail three times.

"Jason."

Moments later, the Goat Man appeared on the other side. He was much smaller and had Jason's eyes.

"Sam."

She couldn't bring herself to embrace him. Not like this, and not so soon.

But perhaps one day, she could learn to love him for what he now was.

Perhaps.

The End

Check out other great

Cryptid Novels!

Hunter Shea

THE DOVER DEMON

The Dover Demon is real...and it has returned. In 1977, Sam Brogna and his friends came upon a terrifying, alien creature on a deserted country road. What they witnessed was so bizarre, so chilling, they swore their silence. But their lives were changed forever. Decades later, the town of Dover has been hit by a massive blizzard. Sam's son, Nicky, is drawn to search for the infamous cryptid, only to disappear into the bowels of a secret underground lair. The Dover Demon is far deadlier than anyone could have believed. And there are many of them. Can Sam and his reunited friends rescue Nicky and battle a race of creatures so powerful, so sinister, that history itself has been shaped by their secretive presence? "THE DOVER DEMON is Shea's most delightful and insidiously terrifying monster yet." – Shotgun Logic Reviews "An excellent horror novel and a strong standout in the UFO and cryptid subgenres." –Hellnotes "Non-stop action awaits those brave enough to dive into the small town of Dover, and if you're lucky, you won't see the Demon himself!" – The Scary Reviews PRAISE FOR SWAMP MONSTER MASSACRE "B-horror movie fans rejoice, Hunter Shea is here to bring you the ultimate tale of terror!" – Horror Novel Reviews "A nonstop thrill ride! I couldn't put this book down." – Cedar Hollow Horror Reviews

Armand Rosamilia

THE BEAST

The end of summer, 1986. With only a few days left until the new school year, twins Jeremy and Jack Schaffer are on very different paths. Jeremy is the geek, playing Dungeons & Dragons with friends Kathleen and Randy, while Jack is the jock, getting into trouble with his buddies. And then everything changes when neighbor Mister Higgins is killed by a wild animal in his yard. Was it a bear? There's something big lurking in the woods behind their New Jersey home. Will the police be able to solve the murder before more Middletown residents are ripped apart?

Check out other great

Cryptid Novels!

Hunter Shea

LOCH NESS REVENGE

Deep in the murky waters of Loch Ness, the creature known as Nessie has returned. Twins Natalie and Austin McQueen watched in horror as their parents were devoured by the world's most infamous lake monster. Two decades later, it's their turn to hunt the legend. But what lurks in the Loch is not what they expected. Nessie is devouring everything in and around the Loch, and it's not alone. Hell has come to the Scottish Highlands. In a fierce battle between man and monster, the world may never be the same. Praise for THEY RISE : "Outrageous, balls to the wall...made me yearn for 3D glasses and a tub of popcorn, extra butter!" – The Eyes of Madness "A fast-paced, gore-heavy splatter fest of sharksploitation." The Werd "A rocket paced horror story. I enjoyed the hell out of this book." Shotgun Logic Reviews

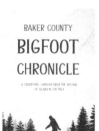

C.G. Mosley

BAKER COUNTY BIGFOOT CHRONICLE

Marie Bledsoe only wants her missing brother Kurt back. She'll stop at nothing to make it happen and, with the help of Kurt's friend Tony, along with Sheriff Ray Cochran, Marie embarks on a terrifying journey deep into the belly of the mysterious Walker Laboratory to find him. However, what she and her companions find lurking in the laboratory basement is beyond comprehension. There are cryptids from the forest being held captive there and something...else. Enjoy this suspenseful tale from the mind of C.G. Mosley, author of Wood Ape. Welcome back to Baker County, a place where monsters do lurk in the night!

Check out other great
Cryptid Novels!

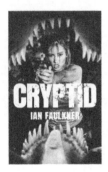

Ian Faulkner
CRYPTID

Be careful what you look for. You might just find it.1996. A group of 14 students walked into the trackless virgin forests of Graham Island, British Columbia for a three-day hike. They were never seen again. 2019. An American TV crew retrace those students' steps to attempt to solve a 23-year-old mystery.A disparate collection of characters arrives on the island. But all is not as it seems. Two of them carry dark secrets. Terrible knowledge that will mean death for some – but a fighting chance of survival for others. In the hidden depths of the forests – man is on the menu. Some mysteries should remain unsolved...

Eric S. Brown
LOCH NESS HORROR

The Order of the Eternal Light, a secret organization have foretold the end of the human race. In order to save all humanity, agents of the Order must locate the Loch Ness Monster and obtain a sample of its blood for within in it is the key to stopping the apocalypse but finding the monster will be no easy task.